The Leasing Agency

CG Edwin

Published by CG Edwin, 2014.

THE LEASING AGENCY

First edition. May 27, 2014.

Copyright © 2014 CG Edwin.

ISBN: 979-8230601975

Written by CG Edwin.

The Leasing Agency
By Larry Chad Lundy (writing as CG Edwin)
Copyright 2013 Larry Chad Lundy
Smashwords Edition

The rocket exploded. Gravity released us. The canvas top tore away....Fire burned my skin. Dust stung my eyes.... We rode the air... The world reversed. The sky was below, the earth above. Aunt Rachel flew away. I held tight...to a bar...to Jasmine.... Gravity pulled back....The desert smashed into us.

They say you can learn a lot about yourself, from what you are thinking about, when they wake you up. That first thing that runs through your mind, when they first bring your brain online, after so long, is an insight to your soul. Mine was the day my father died. I didn't actually witness my father's killing, but as we left him, we knew he was about to die. Moments before, my sister, mother and I were crowded in the back of a covered truck with many current, or soon to be widows and orphans. It was a group of refugees making a desperate attempt to escape a certain slaughter. We were all that was left of a once defiant population bent on revolution. At least I had a sort of good bye with my father. We had shared a glance, before my mother had managed to pull me away. It was more of a farewell than most families had gotten during the revolt's fall. I have no idea what happened to my Aunt Rachel, after she was thrown from the truck. I hope it was a quick death.

Soft music mixed with nature sounds greeted me as I came back to consciousness. My vision was blurred but I could make out the earthy warm tone of the room. This was a definite upgrade from the tiny Spartan cubicle they put me asleep in. Her voice was nurturing and she knew how to comfort with a light touch on your shoulder. This woman was an excellent choice to greet someone who returning to their life after such a long absence. However, comfort wasn't what I was after. I needed to know how long it had been. "Not long" was her first response as I immediately wanted to know. Then she claimed to not know the exact years. The unavailable information was as intentional as the lack of mirrors in the room. There was a well-researched policy on how to handle people like me. A policy I did not care to adhere to. Perhaps most individuals cope better by not focusing on how much of their lives they have missed at first, but I wanted to know before I let myself hope for better news, than was coming.

What can be more familiar than your own body, but mine was, somehow, foreign. I could recognize my hands and arms, but I could see changes immediately. We think of how the years show on our faces, not our limbs, but there was no reflective surface, to see my face. I noticed changes in my skin. I was a little relieved, when I felt the top of my head, to find I wasn't bald. Aging is a slow enough process that it can go mostly unnoticed until reminded by something like a decade old picture. My old picture was the last memory I had.

I pushed relentlessly for the number I required. I surprised myself by the manner in which worked for what I wanted. My own forcefulness caught me off guard. The last words spoken to me had been: "When you wake up, it'll be like you've only slept for a night". I felt deceived as I struggled to orientate myself in this lush recovery room. My last memories felt old, even though I could recall nothing since them. I had never been weak, surviving into my late teens had been no easy feat considering the environment I came to age in. However, being this forceful, with those who had authority, was something I shied away from. I learned the consequences of being an agitator young. My father was an agitator. I was self-aware of all this new behavior, as I remained goal oriented. I knew what I needed to do to eliminate as much of my current vulnerability as I could. Despite the protests from a series of professional care givers, I escaped my private room and apprised my surroundings, replaced my gown with proper clothing and pressed everyone I could find till I got my number......
Fifteen.... I was gone for fifteen years.

I had caused a great amount of stress to a group of people who had just been doing their jobs. Whether or not I was justified in this, I really didn't care. As I noticed all these changes in myself, I was already comfortable with the fact that I was no longer the boy who had gone to sleep a decade and a half ago. These changes would be even more obvious with all the killing I would soon be doing.

I wanted the exercise, to help get my strength back. However, I choose to relent on my insistence to walk the short distance to my housing. I understood the point of the car. They made no attempt to provide you a sense of going home, that was something you had lost forever. Instead, you would be given the experience of the rich on holiday. Riding in the back of a car didn't make me feel important though, it only reminded me of the day my father died. At least it wasn't painful flashbacks. For the first time, it was only a sad memory. I was being taken by limo to luxury accommodations. However, only a few decades before these would have been considered a sedan and a one bedroom apartment. I wasn't old enough to remember when the human race had a high-standard of living, but pictures and movies of this time were still available when I was a child. On my application I had requested to stay at the beach on my leave. Nothing bad had ever happened to me at the beach. I had never been to the beach. They made no guarantees on fulfilling your requests, and therefore I got a scenic view of the woods in the bottom of a valley. This forest was vastly healthier than the ones I had struggled to survive though, so it wasn't too distracting. As soon as I stepped out of the car, I felt eyes on me. When you've been hunted, as much as I had, this is a feeling you come to know well. Could I have picked up on something, or was I just paranoid? There was no reason for me to be spied on. I couldn't have been mistaken as a threat to anyone. I told myself that I was just waking up, the way I went to sleep...."scared." It didn't matter. If someone wanted to watch, so be it. I was planning to give them a boring show.

I was greeted at my suit by Janna. She referred to herself as my personal assistant, as she explained that she would "handle any need that I might have." She gave away her inexperience as she realized how I could have possible interpreted her "handling my needs". Janna corrected, that she would "arrange my needs to be handled." Her blushing face shown a slight offense when I was uninterested by however she was involved in the "handling of my needs". The lessons my father taught, had not left me during my long sleep. As I had done with everyone I encountered that day, I first appraised Janna's potential threat level. She showed every sign of being intimidated by me. Keeping her distance, she offered nothing to hold my attention. "Identify the intentions of the people, then, study the environment". My father's words were as clear, as they were when they were fresh in my ears. The time away from my body had not dulled my instincts. The rules I had been taught as a child, had kept me alive in the camps, and I would continue to follow them. The front door of my "Suite," lead into a sitting area. Straight ahead, beyond a small couch, the kitchen made up the back right corner of the square apartment. The only real walls were to my left, surrounding the bathroom. A mixture of lattice and fabric separated the bedroom and completed the square footage of the living area. Outside, a balcony ran the width of suite, offering a view of the forest. I was on the second floor. I didn't like it. I wasn't that far off the ground, but directly beneath the balcony was a few feet of thick hedges, not good for landing. Beyond them was the hard concrete of the Hotel driveway. If I came under attack from the front door, the back did not offer a quick escape. I almost asked Janna for a different room. Then I realized what I was doing. I had given up so much of my life, so that I could avoid these thoughts. I would force myself to stay here. It did help that only a small railing separated the balconies. I could escape in that manner, if needed.

Janna had a suggested itinerary me. It was another well thought out process for maximizing my mental health. As before, I did not care to follow anyone's script. Arrangements had been made for my family to visit me in the morning, but I meant to go to them now. My temporary luxury wasn't nearly as important as their permanent lifestyle. I wasn't mourning my lost time, but I wanted to make sure my sacrifice had benefited those who I love. Janna attempted to resist my intentions, but I was soon on a train leaving the valley.

The tracks lay at the bottom of a man-made ditch. My first theory was they lowered the cars below ground level, to minimize its target profile, or to lessen collateral damage if a bomb was set off on it. It took a few moments for it to occur to me that it was sunk into the ground only to keep the view of the natural setting, unobstructed. Great effort put forth, only for esthetic purposes, was a foreign idea to me. The inside of the cars were simple, clean and white. There were only small port holes that allowed the riders to peer out. The only item that resembled decoration, were a few monitor screens. Advertisements were running as I boarded. There was a restaurant soliciting diners, two different transport companies competing for travelers, but "The Leasing Agency" dominated the programming. There was a great variety in the manners the company promoted itself. From straightforward recruitment of "Active Participants," to other services they had grown into, such as housing and education, to finally boasts of the positive effects their presence has had on the community. For a "Participant," that didn't want to think about how short his "inactive" time would be, it was beyond overkill. However, I understood that in this environment. There weren't many businesses to advertise. It seemed as though humans, renting their bodies out, for the amusement of an alien race, was the only industry that was booming.

Rising over the ridge, it became obvious why the "privileged" housing was at the base of the mountain. The tracks emerged from the ground and elevated into the air, to rise above the staggered rows of razor wire fence. Descending from the peak we crossed the wall where the lush forest gave way to the slums. I was finally looking at something

I recognized. There were a few more shacks and a lot more tents, but the filthy overcrowded ruins of a dead civilization's former city, were still very familiar to me. There was no landscape here worth preserving. The railway was four stories in the air, to separate the passengers from the anarchy below. The heavily guarded stations were elevated too. The well maintained buildings, stood out among, mostly, dilapidated structures. Soaring high above the wasteland, the view revealed the reason for a commuter train to have so few, and small, windows.

The advertisements were broken up by alerts as soon as the threshold of decay had been crossed. The warnings focused on the "A" zones. There were different terms used before my 15 year break, but I knew what they referred to. The A zones were the secure areas. The gist was that it was a bad idea to leave the A zones. If you did, making it back would be your own responsibility. In order to re-enter, you would have to prove that you were authorized to do so. Your "identification" seemed to be the most valuable possession you could have. It was made clear that it would be required at all "enter/exit crossings." There were also stern warnings regarding anyone else trying to use your identification. There seemed to be no allowance for the other person not having your permission or taking it by force. These conditions didn't concern me. I wouldn't need to leave the A zones to visit my mother. My lifetime had paid for her and my sister to live in the secured areas.

My mother's face was gone. In its place was one that, should have, belonged an elderly relative of hers. She had experienced many lifetimes worth of pain and suffering before I went under. I had hoped that I could have provided relief with my sacrifice, but the aging shown, proved that the turmoil had continued. She was frozen in place, with her hand still on the door she just opened. She knew I was awake and that I was coming. Still, expecting something can't always prepare for it, when it actually happens. I'm sure my changed appearance was as stunning for my mom, as hers was for me. Tears began to roll down her face. She was awkward, unsure of how to move. I moved forward to embrace her and held her as she cried. There was something different about that moment, than I had expected. My mother was happy to see me, but joy was not what she felt. She wept more for what we had lost, than rejoiced for our reunion. She did not speak as we finally gathered ourselves and moved back into the apartment.

More had changed about my mother, than just the way she looked. She was distant, her eyes were hollow. Shock from my arrival, after such a long time away, was understandable, but she seemed to want to hide from me. My return brought pain with it. There was an absence. Someone dominated the room by not being in it. My mother's silence gave me the answer, I just needed the details.

"Where's Jasmine Mom?" I had rarely used my sister's full name. I preferred much more casual nick names like "Jazz" or "Jazzy," but this felt like a formal occasion to me. Mom wanted to escape me, but the tiny apartment left few options with me blocking the front door. The best she could was about 6 ft. The chairs faced each other from across the living room. Mother could have gotten a few feet further if she had went to the back wall that made up the kitchen, but she noticeably needed to sit down. I was desperate to know, but I handled her with gentle patience. At this point, the only people I would have given compassion to were my mother and sister.

"I didn't want her to do it, I didn't know that she would," Mom finally managed. It was the worst that I had feared. I could not use the exact wording my mother used to tell the story. It was a benefit that she told the story out of order and kept repeating herself. In my shock, I was only able to catch pieces of her ramblings. I can only paraphrase the tale now. Their outlook had been positive for the first few years, after I had went under. My contract had gotten them membership to the newly formed A zones, paid for most of the lease of the apartment, provided the tuition for my sister's education, and granted them access to The Leasing Agency's cafeterias and clinics. Despite early reason for optimism, life had remained a struggle. I had sold myself to give them most of the basic necessities, but it was difficult for them to make those last few ends meet. Employment inside the A zones, for former refugees, was demanding and paid little. Jasmine did become qualified for the better jobs, once she graduated. However, those jobs were scarce, and those with her same degrees, were not. I had given up everything, just to get them to the point where they could fight to barely survive.

Then my mother had gotten sick. Her condition was treatable, but not with the basic healthcare that my contract had provided. Her statement of "I was gonna take care of it," meant that she had planned suicide. My mother knew that Jasmine couldn't let her suffer, and she didn't plan to give her the option. The mistake mom made, was hesitating. Jasmine suggested they submit a request to the Agency, to wake me up early. It was a hopeless cause, but Mom decided to take a day to spend it with her daughter. Jasmine showed her the signed contract at dinner. It was done, once the contract was signed, there was no turning back. That was nine years ago, my mother had been alone ever since. I knew now why her eyes seemed hollow. She was empty, life was empty. Her children had given up their lives so that she could spend her last few years, mourning their loss.

Mom tried to minimize the devastation with a few minor positives. My sister's deal was more generous than mine. The family now owned the apartment, and the utilities were covered for decades. Each of us would now receive full food allowances and complete medical care. These were important because Jasmine had managed to get a contract with a guaranteed expiration. This sort of deal had been rumored to be coming when I had joined. My agreement was open ended, it was likely that I would be released if I reached an advanced age, but there was no assurance given. In theory, I could be kept active until I died. Young bodies were much more in demand than the elderly. Just as female bodies were more popular than male. However, there still seemed to be a market for economy "participants." Fees could still be collected for old men. Everyone, like me, signing up, hoped that with the constant influx of fresh young bodies, that the agency would feel motivated to release from our contracts while at least still in our middle ages. However, we all knew when dealing with the Agency, all that really counted was what was in writing. My sister had negotiated a term limit to her contract. She had signed on for twenty-five years. Jasmine could return to her life in her fifties. Of course, there's always a drawback. Her minimum amount of leaves was only one. It was possible that she would get another visit to her body, during that time, but unlikely. As much as the Agency promoted the vacations from duty of the "active participants," they were rare. Even when I joined, it was known that the company worked to limit the amount of off-duty time. Somehow I knew that this practice had only gotten worse while I had been asleep, Mother kept adding to the list of "Pros," but she was working harder to convince herself, than me.

I had seen the apartment once before. We all "moved in" the day I went to sleep. I had hoped to get to spend at least one night there, but the construction wasn't finished before my "report date." Maybe 300 sq. ft., it was barely larger than the tent my family had shared, when my father was still alive. It wasn't a sizable home that I had sought to give them. It was the solid walls and a door with a good lock, which I would give everything to provide. It was clean, obviously obsessive care was taken keeping it so. Pictures hung perfectly spaced on the white walls. The few photographs that had survived through the fall of the revolution had been repaired and reprinted. Most of the images were of my mother and sister after my term began. This was appropriate, it was the first time in our lives that there was time to even think of things, such as keeping memories. My eyes stopped when I came to what was the most recent photo. It was of my sister at The Leasing Agency, the day she went under. She had grown so much since my last memory of her. My little Jazzy, had become a woman…just in time to sell her life away….This would most likely be the last image I would ever get to see of her.

My mother had stopped speaking. She stared quietly at me as I stared at Jasmine's photo. I turned back towards her, but neither of us had any words to speak. Finally she had a suggestion, "we should go out to the courtyard, it's nice out there." Had I not just come from the lush valley, I would have been impressed by the courtyard. It was only a forty by forty area, but it was open with healthy trees and grass. The view was dampened by the constant backdrop of the 15 ft. tall concrete walls that connected the space between two apartment buildings. However, they were a border of the A zone, so not only was there protection necessary , a flat solid color was far more attractive than the slums beyond.

"Your sister loved this place, she would come out here to do her schoolwork" offered my mother. She was uneasy as she sat down on a bench and tried to use her hands to shield her pale face from the sun. I could tell that it had been a long time since she had been out here. It was obvious that even this small open area made her uncomfortable. It had probably been a great deal of time since she had even been outside. With the arrangement my sister had made, Mom could have her food brought to the building. Nothing forced her to leave except the doctors. That was, if she ever had a needed medical attention anymore. The apartment had meant safety to me, a place that could protect my family more than my presence could. Now, instead providing security, it had become a prison for my mother. It was a cell where she could waste away while being reminded of all her regrets. I sat down next to her on the bench. I had nothing to say to her, but at least I could be near her. There was nothing but sorrow and pain from what she told me. The grief stole any joy we could have shared. We remained, seated quietly, for some time.

My mother finally looked like herself, when fear over took her face. I spun to locate the source of danger. A figure was descending down the wall on a rope. It took only a glance to identify this was someone not authorized to be in the A zone. I knew what I should do, what I've always done. I must remove my mother from the situation. The best way to protect her is to remove her from the danger. I was always taught to escape the threat, not face it, unless I was forced. This is what I had always done, but this not what I did. I leapt from the bench, meeting the man as he hit the ground. He produced a metal pipe. I seized it with my left hand and struck him with my right. The second intruder appeared down from us a few feet on the wall. With my second punch, the first attacker released his pipe. I tore the weapon away as I raced towards his compatriot. My aggression caught him off guard; he presented a knife while backing away. I slammed the pipe down on his hand. The blade bounced off the ground. I swung the tube up against his chin. Flipping the pipe, to is jagged edge, I plunged it into his chest. My own force sent me tumbling over the limp body. I righted myself in time to see the first assailant picking up his comrade's knife. He lunged, blade first. I slid to the side, grabbing his right hand and twisting it. I used his own momentum to pierce into his gut. Cranking his hand around, I spun the blade through his organs. These two, were dead or near-death. I scanned the area for more, there were none. Only my horrified mother remained in the courtyard.

The detective's name was Saunders. Saunders' cheap suit told me who he was before he had a chance to introduce himself. He had first tried to speak to me while my mother was still hysterical, but I ignored his questions. Her emotions caught me off guard. She was the one who had taught me how to deal with the aftermath of violence. We had seen so much killing together, why was this so different? Perhaps her new life had allowed her to change? What was only a few days ago for me, had been fifteen quiet, long years for her. At least my life had purchased my mother the chance to become unaccustomed to violence. It took a sedative from the E.M.T.'s to calm her down.

"So you're a rental?" Saunders offered, as he began to puff on his crude cigarette. "Rental" was a slang term, usually meant as an insult. I knew Saunders' game before he even began. I had been dealing with his kind my entire life. Sometimes they wore badges, sometimes they had uniforms, often they drew their authority only from their weapons, but a cop was always a cop. The detective wanted to get a reaction from me, one he could read. I knew what to give him. I knew how to show fear, to give him comfort in his own authority, but not show guilt, to not peak his curiosity. I just didn't care to play along. "Yeah, I just woke up from 15 years, today." I answered in the most combative way I could, while establishing how impossible it would be, for me to be suspicious in any way. Saunders' brushed off my tone with "I know, you're a Eastern Independent right?" It was surprising that he would bring up my childhood in the revolution. The movement had died decades ago. "My dad was, I was just a kid when it fell apart." clarified my role. "You must have picked up something, you took care of those two guys like a trained soldier would." His point was clear and it was a valid one. I wasn't about to show him that I agreed with him, "My dad was killed when I was a boy, you learn to defend yourself, growing up in the refugee camps, with only your mother and little sister." I then turned the direction of the conversation, "How did they get in here in the first place?" Saunders kept his posture of suspicion as he answered "Just a wall, all they got to do is throw up a latter with a rope." This was not satisfying "How can it be that easy? This is an A zone!" The detective measured himself as he answered "It's a low level A zone."

"Budget cuts," became the theme of the rest of our conversation. Armed Guards had once manned every vulnerable area like this open park. As time had progressed, these guards had become less available. The security of the A zones had become a challenge with limited resources. A poverty-stricken populous, seemed to be the only abundance in this society. The line between the civilized and uncivilized was becoming harder to maintain. I frustrated Saunders with a constant barrage of questions regarding the level of "peace" he was actually "keeping." Only part of my motivation was to end the interrogation he was giving me. I had a made a string of disappointing discoveries since waking up, I was enjoying the chance to vent. He had no good answers for me. Realizing that he lacked any good questions for me, he ended the conversation. I was left with a great deal of energy that I needed to express.

The two young women were the perfect metaphor for the world that existed in the valley. They looked nearly perfect.. from a distance. It had become obvious that the only way to avoid disappointment, was to not inspect anything very closely. They were young and attractive, but thick make-up tried to hide numerous scars, while low-light dimmed the malnourished sheen of their skin. At least there was some truth in their beauty, the seduction in their eyes was nothing but an act. I had not requested group sex, I had only requested company. Janna had made the decision for a threesome for me. The one who did the talking made a noble effort to "sell it." Her partner strained to maintain a "come on" look in her eyes. The blonde provided names as part of their introduction. I paid no real attention to what she said. I lacked any interest in learning any false titles.

I wasn't a virgin. I had had sex exactly three times before I went under. I meet Sheila right after the revolution fell apart. We grew up in the camps together. She leased herself out more than a year before I did. Sheila wasn't my girlfriend. There wasn't time for something a trivial as a teenage relationship among refugees. It was not a decision prompted by romantic inspiration. The night following the signing of her paperwork, Sheila concluded that she wished to be in control of her body the first time it had sex. I was the natural choice for her mate. Privacy was scarce among the tents. In the four days we had before she went under, we only managed to be alone long enough for two adult interludes. They were both very quick and awkward. Even as a novice, I could tell that Sheila found them unsatisfying. She did seem to enjoy the way I looked at her following our first time. I was thankful that I could at least make her smile in some way.

My second partner was Mrs. Williams. I never learned her first name. She was only ten or so years older than me, but already a wife and mother, when I meet her. Mrs. Williams became a widow in the camps. Being a single mother, of young children, she was very vulnerable in the camps. She clung tight to the unofficial group that my family was a part of. I had often assisted her and her sons, whenever I could. Often, it had been my mere presence which had provided her the most use. I was far from an intimidating figure, but the mere proximity of a man, made Mrs. Williams and her children less of a tempting target. It had been by accident that we found ourselves alone. I had never seen the expression of her face. My encounters with Sheila had not prepared me to understand the connotation of the "thank you" Mrs. Williams was offering me. I stared at her blankly until she pushed me down onto the cot. I finally caught on, as she mounted on top of me. Beyond my physical arousal, no action was required on my part. It was longer effort than those before, but no more intimate.

My few hasty sexual experiences did not explain the way I set upon the prostitutes. I've always liked women, but this was the first time I expressed my lust so openly. I had never had the time to imagine the acts, must less decide I found them appealing, that I was requesting these girls to perform. I had been displaying so many new characteristics on this day, that I noticed this development, but did not spend much time pondering it. I had a goal to achieve.

I had them start together. I could see the blonde's face. She was a pro. Her moans of pleasure were almost convincing. I had never had access to condoms before. My attempt to read its instructions, must have given the girls the idea was confused. The blonde pushed her partner off of her, and kneeled down before me. She used her lips to slide the condom on. It was my first experience with oral sex. I liked it. It was enjoyable, but I had energy that needed to be used. I lifted her up and guided her back on the bed. As we neared the bed together, she flipped me over, and mounted on top. She seized me with her legs. Slamming down on to me, she took me inside. She pulled up, and came back down hard. I had meant to be on top, but she had taken control. The blonde girl was calling out to me. She demanded the sex graphically. With hands on either side of my face, she directed my attention towards herself. It seemed suspicious to me. I wondered if I had been set up. I forced my head out of her grip, to see what the red head was doing. She was just lying at the foot of the bed. Nude, she was curled up, as if trying to remain covered. Then I scanned up and saw her face. She wasn't crying or noticeably upset, but I could tell what she was feeling, before she had a chance to cover it up. I saw that pain in her eyes. It was a look I had seen many times, on many young faces in the camps. It was the look of a victim. It was the thought of keeping that look off of Jazzy's face, that made signing my lease possible. The blonde wasn't setting me up, she was trying to protect the other girl. The faster she could wear me out, the less the other girl would have to endure. I froze. "Are you okay?" A couple seconds before, she had been screaming: "Fuck me!" now the blonde awkwardly, patted me on the shoulder. I realized I was still inside of her. I pushed her off of me. I wanted to say something. "I'm sorry," was the best I could do. I felt dirty. I headed for the shower. I tried to wash them off me.

It took a moment for me to understand why they were selling me so hard. I had ended it quickly. I was paying for the full session, even the services we didn't get too, and tipping. The blonde had gotten to keep me from touching the other girl, why was she trying to get me to buy a full night? It didn't make sense. If they were here all night, how could they think I wouldn't be able to go through with it at some point? I was finding discomfort with the women now. I wanted to pay them, so they could get out of sight. Of course, they had been told to sell me more time, but they seemed to be very poor negotiators. The price plummeted, as I showed no hint of temptation. Finally, they sweetened the deal to the point where I could not ignore their pleas. The acts would be degrading, but they would cost less than the most basic services. The discount they were offering would be, most likely, more than their percentage of the take. It was not more money they were after, it was a night in the valley. The girls finally had some desire in their eyes, but it was mixed with fear. Whatever they would have to do with me, it would mean being safely positioned in my hotel. The Hell of the slums was so intense, that they would volunteer to be abused by a stranger for free, to avoid it for a night.

I knew their emotions. I remembered the hopelessness and desperation to escape the slums. I realized that I had now fully joined in the cycle of abuse. I had become just like one of the men, who I saw come to the camps.....I stopped the thought in my head. I couldn't handle where the realization was traveling. I agreed to the deal they were offering. We shared an uncomfortable stare, as I searched for a method to serve all of our needs. Finally I arrived at a story. "Listen, I can't get it up, but for that cheap, you can stay till the morning.... cause I want it to look like I fucked you both all night." It was the best story I could come up with for paying to stay, that would allow the girls to relax and try to enjoy their night of safety. The real key for me had been it allowed me not to think any more about what line I had crossed by hiring them in the first place. There was an awkward pause when I claimed impotence. I pointed them to the well-stocked refrigerator, with the story that I didn't care for the food they had given me, so they could eat away. I instructed them to make full use of the bed, as I wasn't sleepy anyway.

The one truth I spoke, was that I was not sleepy. I grabbed the bottle, of whatever alcoholic beverage was displayed on the kitchen counter, and headed to the balcony...... I heard the first true sounds of pleasure, that I had witnessed since being awoken, coming from the prostitutes as they attacked their hastily assembled sandwiches.

My eyes had not inspected the next balcony over, but I knew she was there. Living in the camps, you're never more than a few feet from another person. Instead of interfering with my night of solitude on the terrace, I actually found it comforting to have another person so close. She did not possess my instincts of awareness, of current surroundings. A large gasp was released once she finally noticed my silent presence. The loud sudden noise caused me to react also. "I'm so sorry, you startled me" she offered as an apology. I admitted my own implication in the situation, for not announcing my presence. As her heartbeat appeared to slow, she accompanied a hand to her chest with "I forget that not much separates these suites...... It's the off-season, but I shouldn't assume to not have a neighbor just because this place is almost empty." I exposed my ignorance with "This is the off-season?" She studied me, as I processed the information.

"You're a rental."

She caught herself off-guard by speaking so hastily. Her eyes immediately opened to show the realization of a social misstep.

"I'm sorry, I mean.."

"Don't worry about it, that's what I used to call it.... Hell, it's what I still call it...I guess"

She paused, trying to read my reaction. It was an easy out for me. I had a great opportunity to end the conversation, but I didn't take it. I surprised both of us with "Would you like a drink?" There was a moment of confusion on her face, then a sudden smile. She leapt across the small barrier between our porches and seated herself at the table across from me. Holding out her hand "I'm Elise." I met her introduction with a simple "Ben." Now aware that I was unprepared for a guest, I began to scan for another cup. I turned back to see Elise holding the bottle up, taking a large gulp directly from it. Setting the bottle back down in between us, she revealed that she had deciphered my intentions. "The swill they issue to you isn't really worthy of using a glass." I smiled in agreement as I shot an embarrassed look at my half empty cup.

"I didn't realize this was swill. Compared to the rotgut we had in the camps, this is fine wine."

My mention of the camps stunned Elise. It was the kind of hesitation caused, when someone bluntly mentions an indication that they have experienced a tragedy. I offered no visual hints of how I expected her to act. Looking back, I could see how my blank expression could have left her confused, but this was simply a fact of my life. I felt no reason to treat it otherwise. Elise took a moment to try to read me. Then it was obvious that she came to a conclusion. "Is that why you did it, to escape the camps? I mean, why you leased yourself?" If I had been asked if I wanted to discuss my life and the decisions I had made during it, I would have honestly responded with "no." However, as Elise bravely began to question me about such personal matters, I found it a relief to be open.

I gave Elise an abridged, but very honest version of my story. I spoke of my childhood in the eastern revolution, and then my life in the refugee camps, after the revolt was crushed. I told her how I had struggled to survive the disease, violence, and starvation that infested the tent cities, only to find adulthood had brought even less hope with it. I told her how I had discovered that there was no "honest" work available, if you did not have access to the "contained areas" (That was name used before the classification of "A zones" was applied) The times were desperate and there were no good options. I summed up my decision with: "In order to keep us alive, I was either gonna have to sell my soul or my life. I choose my life. I thought it would give Jazzy and Mom the best chance." The use of my personal names for my family, gave away that I was speaking to myself as much as Elise. The somber tone of my voice revealed just how successful, my attempt to help them, felt like it had been.

"Sorry, I don't mean to pry. I've just never meet anyone who actually lived in the camps before....I've never meet anyone who had leased themselves before either. Which is strange because I've been hearing about leasing for so long now."

I realized that I knew nothing of her, except for her name. However, this was a property owned by the Agency, which offered a theory of her employment.

"So you work for the Agency?"

She squirmed a little, almost as if she was showing shame. The first time Elise seemed to be resisting eye-contact. Finally she explained: "No, I don't, but my father does. He's pretty high up actually... In the off-season, they let some executives have some of these rooms as one of their perks. He couldn't come till tomorrow, but I wanted to get a little alone-time, so I went ahead and came up. It was must have been a mistake for them to put two of the only occupants right next to each other. My dad will probably be pissed once he shows up." Elise stopped as she seemed to think of something. "Dad's not gonna like being next to a rental is he?" I concluded. She offered a semi-sheepish grin. "And he damn sure wouldn't like his little girl talking to one." Her expression assured me that we were on the same page. She offered in defiance: "I am an adult, old enough to decide who she talks to and drinks with.... Don't worry I'm older than I look. I've already graduated college and of legal age to consume alcohol." Her statement reminded me of another adjustment I'd have to make. I tried to play it off with "Legal Age? I never thought about that, being old enough to drink was never an issue in the camps." She smiled in response, but I had not been honest with what I was thinking. I had been open with Elise up to this point, I decided to not change that now.

"You have to remember, you don't look young to me. In my yesterday, I was around your age."

It was going to take me some time to adjust to my new age group. I wondered if I would be awake long enough for that adjustment to occur. Then I wondered if I would ever be awake long enough to get used to what age I would be, again in my lifetime.

"It's probably best to not think about that, if there's any way you can. Even if you're just delaying the inevitable, better to have as many days that you can just enjoy, as possible."

Elise had managed to translate my statement and the quiet introspection that followed it. She knew what was on my mind. It was bold of her to make that statement to someone she had just met. It was what I needed to hear. I instantly agreed with her. I did my best to follow her advice.

"So if you don't work for the Agency, what do you do?"

A fatigued smile appeared.

"I'm a professional applicant at the Agency."

I raised an eyebrow to express my confusion.

"I don't have a job. The closest thing to having a job is working to being hired by the agency. I've had a degree for over a year. I waste a great deal of time taking b.s. classes for "graduate studies," so it doesn't appear that I'm just unemployed. Besides that I keep my dad's apartment exceptional clean and use all the vacation rooms, he's usually too busy to take advantage off...Well, I might find time for some socializing too, but a girl has got to fill her calendar somehow."

I was confused: "You said your father was an executive in the Agency, but he can't help you get a job?" Her fatigue now overwhelmed her smile, "The best nepotism has been able to do me, is entry level in the security department. Which that is actually better than most can do, but that means you're one of the people they send in when things start exploding. My Dad would rather me get drunk with you every night than be sent in to put down an armed uprising..... There's a lot of powerful people out there who have kids, that need jobs. It's almost impossible to start you career inside the valley. It's actually tough to get something that's in a High-level A zone. You've got to put in some time, in a risky area, before they'll consider for a safe gig. Not that there's ever an opening anywhere. Someone would have to die, to get a job working at this hotel."

She forced a smile to return to her face, "Sorry, I didn't mean to rant."

"It's okay, I asked."

It was quiet for moment. We were both searching for something to say, but somehow it was not an uncomfortable silence.

"Would you like to listen to some music?"

Elise smiled at her own inspiration, as she leapt up and crossed back to her suite.

I vaguely remembered the music players, so I knew what the box was, that she returned with. However, I still caught myself staring at the device in awe, as a tap of her hand created sound. "Let's set the mood with something soft and relaxing." With a few more taps on a screen she adjusted the theme. We sat back and were serenaded by the small computer. There would be breaks, where I would regale Elise with stories of refugee camp bands using homemade instruments. She seemed to enjoy hearing of imaginative ways we managed to have the few rustic celebrations among the chaos. Mostly though, we sat quietly in the cool night and listened to her little plastic cube, sing to us. There didn't seem to be a need to talk. As dawn approached, Elise's eyes showed her exhaustion. I suggested she head to bed, but she assured me that she was "fine." Elise then promptly put her head down on the table and fell asleep. I continued to sit and listen to the music, I had slept enough.

I had almost forgotten about the two girls a sleep in my bed, until they began to stir in the morning light. Waking up in a strange room had left them disconcerted. They were taken aback, as I meet them in the doorway. They seemed stunned when I asked how many pancakes they would like.

The smell of hotcakes, eggs, and some form of bacon, broke Elise's slumber. She awoke to a scene that involved me laboring to provide a spread to the prostitutes I had hired the night before. Elise paused a moment, as she arrived at the kitchen bar. I put her plate down before her, she sat down and began to eat without a word.

The fourth call to my mother that morning, was my last attempt. For the first message, I had hoped that she had already gone to the train. I left her a reminder of the details of her valley pass, just in case. I took a basket of fresh cheese to the station with me. I remembered her talking to me as a child about how much she had missed cheese. It was the best arrival gift I could think of. The next two messages were left in between the morning arrivals that she was not on. The fourth and final message was from the apartment. I had already given up on her showing. The cheese was given to a clerk at the train station, who had been eyeing it for the few hours I had waited. I didn't want to try real cheese for the first time, without my mother.

"I'm so sorry, I didn't mean to wake you!"

The shock was blazing on Elise's face. I didn't remember falling asleep. I was half standing now, I must have woke up badly. The sudden dramatic movement, had startled Elise. She was drawing back from me. I tried to calm us both down. "It's okay, I'm sorry if I scared you." We didn't really know each other. There must have been violence in my rising. Perhaps it had reminded this young woman that she was now alone with someone with a background she should be scared of. "I didn't hit you, did I?" Her face relaxed, "No, no I just hate to disturb you, if you were getting some rest." I was glad that she moved back to closer to me. "I've had 15 years to rest, and I'll probably have another 15 here very soon. I don't really want to sleep. Thank you for waking me." Her smile returned, "Well, disturbing people is maybe the one thing I'm good at." She didn't give time for an awkward silence. "Are you alone?" Only then did it occur to me that I had invited Elise over to meet my mother the night before. I didn't have to fight back any emotion. I was still numb. "I got stood up." She couldn't avoid this awkward silence. Although her face read much more empathetic than awkward. "Well, if it makes you feel any better, I was stood up too." Her smile and some levity were exactly what I needed at that moment. "Your dad get stuck working?" "It's possible, but probably busy with some girl about my age who actually thinks he might take care of her." This situation was something she accepted without any visual reaction. Elise moved on quick, "Wanna get some dinner with me?" I nodded without delay; I didn't need to think about it.

I had to fight the desire to use all the cover the trees provided. I did not believe there were any attackers to be weary of. I wasn't concerned about people, I wanted to hide from all the possible hidden positions the surrounding woods offered. I had changed in many ways, but I was still the man whose survival training had begun with his father, before he could remember.

Walking was Elise's idea. I could see where a stroll through the forest could be an enjoyable experience for some. The best I could manage was not letting my mania disturb the journey to much for Elise. I hoped conversation would offer a distraction for me:

"So what is your degree in?"

"Law, unfortunately."

"I assume Corporate Law, to help you get hired at the agency?"

Elise stopped and gave me a confused look. I could her face change, as she reminded herself.

"Oh wow, I forgot. You said fifteen years, right?"

"Yes, that's how long I've been out."

"Well, Corporate Law is really the only form of law now. About ten years ago, The Agency mandated that they were the highest authority."

More of my father's words ran through my head now. I interrupted Elise:

"There code of conduct is binding to all. This applies to anyone on company property, which is where ever they decide it is. It also includes any person, representatives of the corporation, and come in to contact with during the operation of business. If you don't work for the company, they use some term like: Inactive associate or sub-contractor, and process it like an H.R. situation. Only dismissal isn't an option, but incarceration and execution are?"

Elise was confused again:

"Well, they use much more "legal" language than that, but that is what it roughly translates too. Have you been told about it, since you woke up?"

"No, it's something my dad said would happen. He talked about it all the time in Government and History class. It was one of the ways he justified rebelling against the corporations."

"Your father was a teacher, in the revolution?"

"In between battles, yes. He considered regular schooling, for the children, vital to the revolution. He said that we can win our freedom with guns and bombs, but we won't be able to keep it, without an educated population..... He once had an English class meet in the medical tent, because he had taken too much shrapnel, to come to us. He was literally being stitched up, while listening to oral essays."

"Damn, I bet it was hard to impress somebody who was getting cut on. How did you do?"

"Shitty, I had to go before the pain killers kicked in. The last couple of kids got off easy. Dad was a light weight when it came to meds. He actually cried over a paragraph this kid wrote on shapes in clouds."

Elise laughed out loud, and bumped into me playfully. I don't believe she found my story, that funny. I think she was just relived that the conversation had not gone to a darker place. I know, that is why I was smiling.

Elise was very proud that we would be dinning at an "independent" restaurant. Apparently it had become very chic to patronize any business that was not directly owned by the Agency. Of course the vast majority of money that was spent at such institutions came from paychecks issued by the Agency, but at least some found a way to earn a living other than renting bodies.

The building had been a bunker at some point before. Great effort had been put in visually erasing that past. However, I knew why there were so few windows and the need for such thick sturdy, walls. The ambiance had an effect on Elise. She seemed even more invigorated by the setting as we entered. I had never eaten food, which had had so much effort put into its presentation. With my first bite, I discovered that not all the care had been spent on the way it looked. The flavors ignited in my mouth. Most of the pleasure I had received from food in my life, came from the dampening of hunger pains. Now, though, I understood the appeal of gluttony. The intensity of my reaction, must have been blatant on my face, as I looked up to see Elise watching my with a wide grin. She began to enlighten me about what set these offerings apart, from all the food I had consumed in the past. We had a conversation. A conversation that didn't involve refugee camps, the revolution, the leasing agency, the time I had lost, the family I had lost, not even a mention of the act of sleep.

Having gorged ourselves to the brink of sickness, we decided not to walk back to the hotel. Elise took my arm and led me to where the transports stopped, to pick up us lazy travelers. She kept her armed affectionately entangled with mine, as we rode back through the forest. I was too interested in her stories of the places she had seen, to concern myself with how vulnerable we could be. I wanted to absorb every detail she offered about the sandy beaches, to scan the darkness for danger. I was comfortable, warm and relaxed, as we approached the hotel steps.

Elise stopped and withdrew her arm from mine. As I turned to face her, I could tell she had something to say. Once again, she came right out with what she had to say: " Ok, this is the part where we head up to your hotel room and spend the night together, but I'm sorry I can't do that. You had a room full of hookers just this morning, and I can't follow that, 12 hours later." My warmth was gone. Sex had not even registered for me, but I found her disapproval painful. It was hard to breath. Even Elise seemed pained by it: "Wait, I didn't mean it to sound that shitty. I'm not saying that I could never get over that. You did just wake up after 15 years. I would want to get laid too....It's just right now... tonight... Damnit, I just screwed up our good night with that didn't I?..." Her reaction to her own statement, helped my feelings. The way she was feeling, couldn't be helped, but we both wished that wasn't the way things were. This meant there was hope that those feelings could change. This was enough for me. I interrupted her struggle to find the right words. "Will you meet me in the lobby for breakfast in the morning?" Caught a little off guard, she responded with a quick "Yes." With a large smile, I left her with:" Great, see you then." We shared a warm look, and went our separate ways.

I continued to lack the desire for sleep, only it was with a new emotion now. I guess you would say that I was "giddy." I'm not completely sure what it is to be "giddy", only that I had never been it before. I had a strange energy, which seemed as unfocused as it was motivating. I found myself strolling around the three little compartments of the suite, not really doing anything, but completely content in my actions. In fact, I resisted engaging in a task, as it might distract from this activity that I was so enjoying.

So lost in the haze I was in, that the sirens didn't even register at first. The two patrol cars shrieked as the descended upon the hotel. Finally, the pressure on my ear drums, awoke me from my day dream. I could see their flashing lights down to the right from my balcony. I knew something was terribly wrong, but I did not want to let go of this new emotion I was feeling. The burst of yellow, from the distant explosion, washed away all the warmth that I had found. The fireball rose off in the horizon. Instinct told me to get off the balcony. I was slow. The force of the wave hit me as I backed away from the rails. The building itself, trembled as the new explosion sent the police cars tumbling through the trees. I landed on a, no longer solid, floor. I was deaf, except for words my father had spoken to me, long ago. He was teaching me about guerilla warfare. How to split up the enemies forces, when attacking inside territory they hold. "Make the first attack a distraction, to make the goal an easier target. If you can, hit the very assets, they would use to stop you." For some reason, this ran through my head, as I struggled to gain control of my body. The war had found me again. My ear dumbs managed to pick something up, under the high pitched squeal. I heard the shouting and small arms fire down the hall. They were here, but why? Why a building full of rentals? They were only yards away now. I made it to my feet, as it came to me.....They were here for Elise.....

The walls were thin. I could hear them bursting into her apartment. I was on my feet, then over to her balcony. Elise was leaping over her bed, towards me. He was chasing behind her. The glass was cracked from the bomb, I exploded the glass door as I flew through it. I collided with the man. We fell on Elise. A second man charged us. He led with the bayonet that tipped his rifle. I caught the AK-47, by the stock and directed over me. I shoved the weapon back at him. His finger caught the trigger. Automatic fire filled the air with the debris, as it tore through the wall and ceiling. A mass of bodies, we fought sloppy. The magazine spent, I hammered the rifle backwards. I smashed into his face, with the butt on his gun. He stepped back. Elise scratched the man between us, as I lifted myself off the bed. The standing man covered his face. He left his leg exposed. I shattered his knee with a kick. I ripped Elise's attacker off her. He had a pistol tucked in the back of his belt. I used it to blow his lungs out through his chest. More figures appeared in the doorway. I fired two shots to halt their advance.

These were not soldiers. These were well-armed amateurs. They had used guns. They had killed, but they had not been trained how. I held Elise behind the bed. Its sturdy frame offered the best cover. Our adversaries had too much adrenaline. They couldn't remain covered. Their plan had fallen apart; I had a moment before they could regroup. There was no easy route of escape though. Too many guns blocked us in front, too steep a drop to our rear. My suite offered the least blocked path.

Two crude grenades hung on the body that lay on the bed. A man in a trench coat exposed himself; he was punished with a round in his shoulder. The man with the broken knee, fought to reload his rifle. I thanked him for the readied weapon, with a bullet to the throat. More automatic fire sailed past me. They were smart enough aim away from Elise, but needed me dead. I emptied the pistol, and tossed the first grenade. A wave of blood crashed through the kitchen, as a limb was torn loose. I shoved Elise the shattered door, as I tossed the second explosive behind. We sailed over the railing, as pieces of the room flew over the balcony.

We came back to our feet, as I saw my front door buckling. It was being kicked down. The balcony opposite of Elise's was too far to jump. I only had one clip for the rifle. We only had thirty shots for protection. It wouldn't be enough to hold them off. Nowhere to run. No good place to defend. I had to deal with the threat now. I shoved Elise towards my bed with: "Stay down!" I raised the AK-47 to my shoulders. I pulled the trigger with my first step. I pushed the rifle towards the door. It punched hard, back at me. Wood fractured, drywall imploded. My barrage devoured the entrance way. Bullets were getting through, but were they hitting anyone on the other side? A machine gun allows you to fire many shots quickly, but that means you empty quickly. I was racing my own ammunition across the apartment. I didn't know how many men were beyond that door, but I knew the gun would be empty when I got there. I let off the trigger, as I leapt the couch. Stepping over, I opened back up. There was BANG, then CLICK. The last casing dropped to the floor. I took another step and launched myself at the door. I extended my right leg and kicked. The frame gave way. It landed against a hidden figure. First the rifle was a spear. I sank it into a retreating man's throat. Ripping it back out, a trail of blood following, I made it a club. The black hood offered little protection, to the next man's skull. The impact loosened his grip on his handgun. I pulled it free and flipped it around. Two shoots in one man; a knife in the next. One round in another. I stabbed blindly, as I kept firing. Four men lay on the ground. I fired into them, until I ran out of bullets. The last rounds, were into dead men. All went quiet after that last shot.... I stood in silence for a few minutes. I listened for more movement. There was none....until I heard Elise move. She came out into the open slowly. She beheld a full view, as I stood amongst the gore that I had used four men to produce.

****

CHAPTER 2

The Aliens are a secret that everyone keeps from no one. They aren't discussed openly. They are never mentioned by name. That is, if you consider: "The Aliens," a name. I don't know if they've ever been given another title. No one can agree on how contact was made. Some profess that they came here in physical form. "Majestically, floating down through the clouds, they arrived aboard a luminous golden vessel." If this is anywhere near true, it would, most likely, mark the sole occasion they were here in person. The laws of physics make space travel difficult, no matter how technologically advanced, a life form you are. Believers claim that they journeyed here aboard a sort of space ark. Where generations lived and died in order to explore the galaxies. Others say we were discovered by an unmanned probe. It brought the device that let us communicate with them. Another theory is that it was us, that found them. Our own technology advanced to the point where we could see their signal. Whatever the circumstances were, it is that signal, that is key. The signal lets us communicate with them over the vast distance that separates us. It is what allows them to control our bodies.

Depending on your point of view, the Alien arrival either sent, or coincided with human society's fall into chaos. There are those that believe the aliens are malicious, and chose to play games with us. Setting cultures against each other, providing knowledge that would lead to war and chaos. My father taught me it was our reaction to the aliens that caused the collapse. While some proclaimed them gods, others saw them as a threat to their own religion. The world went to war again. As Mankind has always done, we set about committing our greatest sins, in order to prove that our beliefs were the most righteous. Some were just greedy, and sought to use, the Aliens, to gain some sort of advantage. Just as he put such a great importance on my command of language, mathematics, and war strategy, my father filled me with knowledge of his view of history. It was this passion, that led him to join the Eastern Revolution. A decision that had a price so high, that it could not be paid with his own life. It was a debt that his children were still paying on.

I didn't expect Saunders to walk into the room. I knew an interrogation was coming. The response to the attack had been quick and massive. All sorts of uniformed people had descended on the battered hotel. I just didn't think I would recognize who they sent for me. Saunders had much more spring in his step, than when we had meet. He had a bottle in one hand, and two cigars in the other. He shot me a friendly smile. I gave him no reaction. I had been alone in a small, private dining room for two hours. Elise and had been separated by the police, as soon as they arrived. She had to be forcefully pulled from my side. She only became willing to leave me, when I reacted to their hands on her. For the sake of maintaining the peace, she was able to keep her wits and diffuse the disagreement . They put me in a room with no windows, and placed an armed guard outside of the only door.

Saunders was openly cheery, as he poured two glasses. "Benjamin, you must be the most unlucky... and deadliest, son-of-a-bitch, I have ever met!..." He had an open grin, as he shot his eyes up at me. I offered nothing but a stone face. Undaunted, Saunders continued: " this is good for me, because they were willing to buy that I needed good wine and cigars to gain your trust!..." Getting a suspect drunk was an old trick. We both knew I was a suspect. He couldn't think I was dumb enough to fall for the old move. Maybe that was his game. Could Saunders be trying to fill me with confidence? He could play as if we were both above the old cat and mouse. Saunders might want me thinking that he didn't suspect me of anything. I knew I had nothing to hide, but that didn't mean that I would be innocent when it was all over. There would need to be someone to blame for this. This was close to where the rich and powerful lived. There would need to be someone to punish for this. A rental who would soon be locked away, anyway, would be a temping candidate. I would have to handle myself carefully.

He admired the bottle as he caressed it at the same time. Then, moving the bottle into his right, he took a cigar in his left. His eyes went from one to the other: "Hell, I don't know which to get on first!...Alright, here's the thing though, we have to make this seem legit. I told the guard to move down the hall, but we're gonna have to sound heated some, to sell it." Was this part of the sell? Was he making sure that I understood, that he didn't suspect me? Saunders seemed to be going out of his way, to make sure I understood. My only response was: "They brought you all the way here to interrogate me, because you met me the other day?" "Yelp, they're that desperate! Which is good for me, cause I know you were just in the wrong place, at the wrong time." Well, now he had put it as obvious as he could. His joy and relaxation came of as completely genuine. Of course, it could be an act, but I doubted that Saunders was skilled enough to be this effective.

He presented me with the other cigar, he seemed elated, when I shook my head no. Hastily, it was stuffed into his jacket pocket. Saunders first puff on his cigar, was taken at the slowest rate, it was possible for a human to breath. His eyes rolled back in his head, as he slouched down in his chair. After a few quiet moments, he finally spoke. "Ok, so when and where did you learn to be such a bad ass? Cause, I know you have to be tough, to grow up in the camps, but damn!.... It's like you did some action movie shit here!" It was a good question. To be honest, I didn't have a good answer. I would have to offer up the same reason I had given before. "My father taught me how to take care of myself, before he died. I practiced that skill defending my mother and sister in the camps" I retorted. I wanted out of the room. I was more aggressive than I meant to be. I didn't seem to be fully in control. This was dangerous. I would have to give him something to leave. Saunders reacted to my course tone: "You can stop being so suspicious, I checked you out, before I walked in here. You see, working in the city, we've got shit for resources. I have to suspect everybody, and rely on my wits. However, this is the valley. When something goes down in the valley, they give you access to everything." Saunders enjoyed another taste of his cigar. " I researched you. In the fifteen years you've been asleep, most contacts you could have had, are either dead or hooked up to a machine at the agency.... Everybody else you knew, was either in diapers then, or is wasting away in some crazy old person's home." Saunders reacted to his own last statement. He might have realized that he had just made a reference to my mother. It could have been genuine regret for being rude, then again, he may felt it was a misstep in an interrogation. He moved quickly: "Honestly it doesn't matter, this operation was fucked up so bad, who cares who was behind it." I choose to speed up the pace of the conversation: "They care, because they might come after her again." Saunders shook his head: "Nah, she's useless to them now." "Why?" "She wasn't really the target, they only wanted her to get to her daddy.... Only problem is, they screwed up, and killed him." My surprise was not hidden "Yeah, he was standing near the bomb they used to take out those two valley cop cars. Found his hand, with the phone still in it, about fifteen feet from his head. They haven't found much of his lower body yet."

I was focused on offering no reaction, but the information caught me off guard. The conclusion had made sense. Why would a group of armed men stage such an attack to grab an unemployed graduate student? Of course it was because she was the daughter of an executive. It was not that I had not figured it out, it was that I had not tried. I had been solely focused on the next step. I just wanted out of that room, and back close to Elise. Saunders took another drag off his cigar. "These executives are all like sharks, none them are gonna care about this dead guy's daughter.... If you hadn't saved her, she would have ended up with a bullet to the head, or as a sex slave. That's the only use she would have had....." The speech was broken for large gulp from his glass. " By the way, why the hell did you take on seven armed men for her, you couldn't have met her before yesterday.... how good are the blow-jobs?" I gave him a reaction that he could read. It was a mistake, I showed an attachment to her. Not that the nights events shouldn't have revealed my feelings, but , I knew better than to confirm them that easy. Saunders read my expression. He threw his hands up in surrender. "Sorry, I didn't mean anything by it. Just making conversation among guys." Saunders moved to defuse the mood. He set the bottle down with: "Oh hold on, I gotta keep the show going." With that, he stood up moved to, and faced the door. "You have to know something! You're the only one still alive!" The detective stood and listened for a reaction. After a moment, he sat back down and continued to drink.

"Who do you think did it?" I could claim that I was just trying to move the conversation along, but really I needed to know. Saunders shrugged, "One of the gangs." The four words seemed sufficient to Saunders, but they were not enough for me. "A street gang managed to get a couple of bombs, and then get them past all the Agency security?" Saunders was unphased by my challenge. "When I say gangs, I don't those little thugs that used to stir up shit in the camps. These guys took the place of the militias. They don't hide out in the wastelands, they set up shop inside the city....Hell, they are the city." The Militias were Para-military groups made up of left over soldiers from the revolutions. They had been what made the camps an option, people would actually choose. As bad as the camps were, being at the mercy of the Militias was worse. I pressed Saunders: "These gangs are that organized?" He shot me a half grin while taking another drink. "Organized? Nah, they're just ruthless. " He smiled as a man who was proud of his own knowledge. "All these important people here in the valley wanna think that they're safe inside these mountains. They're all real proud of how smart they are. But they've done something real stupid." Saunders leaned towards me as if he was about to share a secret, but he didn't manage to lower his voice. "They brought the gangs in themselves!........ You think they let the workers live inside the fences? Hell no! They bring the laborers in from the city! The gangs touch everything in the city! Your maid may act like she's scared of you, but she's really worried about those animals you send her home to every night!"

Saunders continued his rant. He described his theories of how it would have been easy for the gangs to get in. He painted the gangs as force that couldn't be stopped. They were vicious and well-armed. Many had been taught skills from those who fought in the revolution. He was describing the bombings as "overkill" something that belonged in an ambush, not a kidnapping. That's when his eyes shot up, back at me. For the first time during the interrogation, he showed suspicion. I had to say something to break the train of thought. "What will you do about this?" It wasn't a great line, but it was the only question I had. From Saunders' expression, it seemed to work. He relaxed his eyes and shrugged his shoulders. "Kill a bunch of people." Another drink brought the grin back to his face. "They won't give me grief about wanting man power now. All I'll have to do is point and they'll be raiding the shit outta any place I want!" "Will it do any good?" My question washed the color off of Saunders' face, "No." Without him spelling it out, I could piece the information together from the details he had already given me. Killing some gang members wouldn't stop the problem. They were a result of the problem, not the cause.

Saunders didn't mention Elise again. He kept the conversation light. It could have been an effort to steer me to being compliant. Saunders seemed to be putting much effort into making this a friendly chat. I was not offered another drink, but the wine was steadily consumed. Halfway through the bottle, the detective's demeanor changed. There were no more questions to me. No more discussion of the night's events. He talked about himself; the condition of his own life. It was a dark picture that he was painting. Saunders' eyes were aimed at the wall to my right. He wasn't looking at anything though. He was looking beyond everything in that room. He began to tell his story. It didn't seem to be for my sake. Perhaps he was trying to come to grips with his own opinion. Saunders showed little hope for the world he saw. The speech had a theme: "Worse." Everything was getting "worse." It was his job to maintain order in the city, but Saunders could feel control slipping further away, each day. At first, he had appeared to find humor in violence having made it way to the valley. Saunders seemed to enjoy the privileged having some idea of the suffering he saw constantly. However, as the night wore on, he showed fear that the chaos had found its way, to the last safety. He ended with talk of his family. He struggled to show anything but dread for his son's future. Saunders explained that he struggled to with a way to deal with his wife's desire for more children. It was obvious what his concerns were, but even having spoken so openly, he could not speak the words, that would spell out what he was thinking. He held the empty bottle quietly for a moment. Saunders put the bottle down on the table, and left without speaking anything more. The interrogation was over.

I had proof that I was being watched now. Mostly it was just someone standing just outside the room. Other times a uniform would just walk through the open doorway and make eye-contact with me. No one had asked any questions, since Saunders had left. Elise slept with her head on my lap. She had be groggy when she was released to me. Sedatives seemed to be a common method of dealing with shock. A disconcerted Janna, had made an appearance, once the police opened the scene. She had a difficult time piecing together a sentence. In between mumbling, she pointed me to the back suite we were in, and a promised to "work on other accommodations." It was quite in the room. The sound of Elise breathing dominated. There was a light background of a team of investigators, rustling through the rumble. Mostly, it was private.

I'm not sure if I had ever fallen asleep. Elise hadn't moved, but I knew she was awake. I could feel her eyes scan the room. Slowly, she raised herself up. I had nothing to say, so I just looked at her. Finally, "It all really happened, didn't it?" I nodded yes. With that, Elise looked away, and stared at nothing for a while. She turned to me as if she meant to speak. The words just didn't come from her mouth. It was if, she meant to say something. Something that seemed the appropriate thing to say, but it was just not something Elise would ever say. She was who she was, and that is what she had to be. A sigh showed that Elise resigned herself to what she was capable of. Then she spoke:

"There is no, thank you, I have that is worthy. No way, I can ever hope to repay you. That doesn't mean that I'm not willing to try. I will, gladly, do anything you ask. "

No emotion invaded her words, but they were not cold either.

"For your sake, you should get rid of me quickly. All I bring is trouble. Keep me around, and I'll ruin your life."

It was spoken as if it was an accepted truth. My answer was as matter of fact:

"I don't have a life to ruin"

We sized each other up for a moment. Then I broke the silence:

"Do you want me to take you home, to your family?"

I had found the topic that was on Elise's mind. It took some time for her to find the ability to say it.

"My father was the only family I had.... I lost everything with him.... I have no home to go home to."

She responded to the confusion on my face.

"I won't inherit his apartment. It will be reissued to another executive. I won't receive any of his assets. That's how the agency works.... It's what Dad did when his coworkers died. They won't treat me any better..... I don't have anywhere to go."

She was blunt, so was I.

"I can give somewhere for a few days. For whatever time I have left. Worry about after that, then."

After a moment, she gave a simple "Ok."

I was shocked when Janna fulfilled her promise of alternate accommodations. She was quite pleased with herself when she handed me the keys to one of the cabins that surrounded the lake at the bottom of the valley. Perhaps in time, Janna would not take the needs of rentals, so seriously, but this was a welcome change for Elise and I. Elise had given up all effort, to make me feel able to leave her. She stayed close to my side till we entered the front door of our new lodgings. It was very much a lover's suite. Only a small closet-like room, where the toilet was located, offered any privacy. I could see Elise's form through the curtain that surrounded the shower. I felt it was no invasion, to gaze upon her, as she had undressed in the room with me. Her nudity was not presented as a show. She took her clothes off as if they had felt heavy and constraining on her. Nor did I watch her bath herself, for sexual arousal. Elise was just all I wanted to look at. I did not look away from her as she emerged from the bathing area. The only covering she had was a towel, that was wrapped around her wet hair. As appealing as her body was, it was her eyes that held my gaze. Elise made a last attempt to wring moisture from her hair, then let the towel fall by her feet. She stood before me, with only a few beads of water to cover her skin.

In most cases, it takes years for two people to learn to communicate without talking. At the least, that bond should require more than the matter of days that Elise and I had known each other. However, as she presented herself in front of me, I knew exactly what she meant. Her bare body, was not a sexual invitation, nor was it a rejection. When she slid herself onto the bed, she wanted me beside her. Neither of us wanted anything between us. I peeled my clothes off, as I moved in beside her. Elise raised up slightly, allowing me under her. She laid her head upon my chest, as I curled her up in my left arm. Elise bore down tight upon me. She crossed her ankles as she wrapped around my left leg. She sunk her nails into my right shoulder, as I could feel her tears fall on my chest. Elise was finally letting her emotion out. I could feel her most intimate of skin on my upper leg. I found her body enchanting, but ,me inside of her, wasn't something either of us wanted at the moment. Somehow, that would have felt less close. We kept each other warm, as the cool breeze blew off the lake. Rain began to dance on the tin roof. Time seem to move at a different pace for us.

"It's all my fault…. my father is dead because of me." Elise spoke these words, and then took a bite of food. It was the first thing she had said, since we had arrived. She had slept mostly, when awake, she had silently watched the lake. There was a restaurant, just down the path from our cottage. For a fee, they would walk your order to you. I wanted to stay naked inside, more than I wanted to save the money. I had them bring over an impressive spread. Variety gave a better chance of there being something appealing to Elise. Also, it gave me an opportunity to experience more types of food. I set a tray down in front of Elise with: "I know what you feel, you don't want to eat, but you have to. When my dad was killed, I didn't want to eat, but my mother told that was stupid. Starving myself, only hurt me, it didn't honor my dad, he wouldn't want that. She was right, you have to make yourself eat. You're not some weak little girl, so mourn with a full stomach." She paused for a moment, then showed her agreement by picking up her utensils and at least, attempting, to appear to eat.

Elise had mostly moved her food around the plate, before she made her statement. I wasn't shocked by what she said, but I did stop eating. After swallowing, she turned and faced me. "I was a stupid little girl in college. I fell for a whole lot of bullshit rhetoric. At first, I just ended up in bed with guys who talked big, but just wanted to get high and laid. Then I started looking for someone who would actually do something. I got turned on by the idea of danger, because I really didn't know what danger was…. They talk about changing things, about saving the world. I wanted to be as important, as everybody treated them…. I didn't want them looking at me as a piece of ass, so I bragged about who my daddy was. I actually had myself convinced, that they would use a connection inside the agency, as a tool to make things better....That's the thing though, nobody wants to make things better, they just want power. ...It took a couple of years, but I got hooked up with some of the gangs from outside the A zones. I made a couple of connections with some really dangerous people. That's when I started to finally see what was going on.... These guys would talk about how many children, the agency was letting starve. The whole time, they were pimping those kid's mothers out, while eating seconds in front of them. They saw me as a source of guns, bombs, and better drugs to push. The Agency was just the bad guy, they used to rally everyone behind them. I figured it out, just before they had me convinced to meet outside of the A zone. "

"Is that way your dad didn't want you to leave the valley?"

"Yeah, he didn't tell anyone else. We would have both been arrested if anyone else knew I had been meeting with the gangs.....He thought he could keep me safe."

"How do you know it was the people from your past?" I didn't mean it as a question to comfort her. I was looking for her proof.

"People were trying to contact me, friends from college. People that didn't really have a reason to be working that hard to find me...... Agency security advised my father that his name had been mentioned outside the A zones. Dad thought we'd be safer getting out of the apartment for a while....They were looking for me....They found me" With that, Elise began to eat.

My mother did not answer my calls. There were no phones in the bungalows. I had to travel down a path to a small building to get to one. On the fourth trip, I was unable to force myself to speak when it came time to record a message. I tried to make myself worry about her safety. I wanted to believe this was a sign that she could be in danger. But I couldn't. There was no reason to leave another message. I couldn't help her. I couldn't save her. The best thing I could do, was leave her alone.

I don't know how long the receiver beeped at me, before I noticed and hung it up. I don't know how long I stood there afterwards. The gears in my mind were trying to move. Maybe, whatever they do to shut off your brain, was still having its affect. Maybe all this time, I hadn't been fully awake yet. Possibly, I had managed to remain in denial up until this point. Whatever the case was, I was coming to a conclusion, but it was one that was hard to process. I stormed back to my lodgings and burst through door. The way she began to speak instantly, showed Elise had been waiting for me. "Let's do something, let's get out of here..." I interrupted her: "How long do I have?" I followed with the details before she could ask. "They promised at least a day for every year you're under! So I should have fifteen to start, then an amount they don't tell you, so you don't worry about it. But something tells me I'm not getting it, am I?" Elise had never heard anger in my voice, but that didn't seem to be what bothered her. I had found another subject that was on her mind, that she did not want to face. She didn't shy away though: "Probably not fifteen." My voice quieted some: "How many?" Elise's words seem to hurt as they came out. "They gave my dad a bonus for it.... The program that cuts the off-time. He set up a team that looks for reasons to end off-duty early. It saved a bunch of money for the agency." I couldn't speak, but she knew I needed to know more. "Any excuse will do. Get arrested, leave the A zones, or sometimes just discourage someone else to sign up to be a rental, and they will cancel your leave." I didn't need to say it, but I did: "Something like getting caught up in a gun fight when your hotel explodes?" Elise confirmed: "They may admit that it's not your fault, and say that they'll give you another leave soon, but they're not gonna let a rental and a homeless girl stay where the executives' vacation for long."

I had been angry when it occurred to me, but the confirmation took me to somewhere else. Heat erupted in the center of my chest, and spread outward. My skin burned, and then I lost feeling. I began to move about, but the motions had no purpose. I trembled as I paced. I had been numb since I woke up, but I had not lost emotion, it had just been too intense for me to process it. The pain, I had went to sleep with had only been building for the last fifteen years. Instantly, something else had to feel the intensity I was. My hand was on a chair. Immediately, it was in the air, and then slammed back down again. It was thoughtless violence. Wood splintered and flew, as I crashed the chair down over and over again. I was yelling something, not sure if it was even a language. I could not keep anything inside anymore. Words poured out: "It was for fucking nothing! Fucking nothing!" I pieced together every vulgar word that I knew. I found myself kneeling above a pile of dismembered furniture. I vocalized a new conclusion: "That's all I can do...I can only break things. I just fucking break everything!" My insane display had not scared Elise off. She had held her ground and now she spoke up. "You saved my life! You sacrificed everything for your family! That's not breaking anything!" She didn't understand. I had to correct her: "I didn't save you, I killed them!" I stood, turned and screamed my point to her. "I can kill! I've gotten real fucking good at that somehow, but I can't save you! They're gonna turn my damn brain off any minute, and then I can't do shit for decades!" She was determined to express her point "You gave me a chance...."

"I couldn't protect them!"

My voice broke with the last word. It was the first time I had ever been able to speak it, aloud. Now that I had started talking, I couldn't stop. . "I couldn't keep them safe! So I give up and sell my fucking self, because I know it's the only way I'm ever gonna be of use to them, and what the fuck happens? I wake up to find out that I fucked that up too! My sister is hooked up to some damn machine, while some fucking alien plays in her dreams! My mother is some crazy old woman who won't even talk to me!" My voice was cracking. The words just shrieked out of my mouth. I had held these feelings in for so long. I had hated myself, for not being able to protect my family, for as long as I could remember. They had lived in fear, because I was too weak . No matter how many men I had killed, I was still helpless. "Those guys after you were dumb asses! I managed to kill them, but what the fuck can I do for you now? Not a God damn thing!" I was livid, and no longer in control. Elise could see it. All attempts at civility had been thrown aside between us. I was boiling inside, the pressure had to be released. A craze shown in Elise's eyes as she barked back at me: " Stop screaming and fucking do something!"

I charged Elise and seized by the hair on the back of her head. I forced her lips to mine. There was nothing gentle about it. Our mouths were wild as we came together. Elise bit down hard on my bottom lip. Blood ran free as she pulled back. There was distain in her voice with: "I'm not looking to just make out!" I grabbed her by the ass, and lifted her in the air. I brought her chest up to the level of my head. Tearing open her robe, she pulled my mouth to her breasts. I tried to drink her in, as I carried her towards the bed. At the foot, I tossed her down on mattress. Her legs spread apart as I crawled above her. Elise's right hand slid down between her thighs. She went to work on herself, as she helped tear at my clothes with her left hand. As soon as my pants were down, she seized me with her legs. A violent left hand grasp my face, as her right pulled me inside her. Her voice was wild: "You're good at breaking things? Show me! Try and break me!" I forced all the way in. Elise's back arched to the point where she came off the bed. She gasp out loud, as she shook. An open hand struck me across my face. "Again Damnit! Don't stop!" She moved her hips to guide my strokes. We worked together in a cycle. I held nothing back for her, it was almost an attack. Elise fought me with her hands and nails. Our breathing was strained as we found our bodies limits. Sweat poured to where it helped us slide across each other. Her fingernails split my skin, crisscrossing the claw marks she had just made. I pressed my hands into the bed to push myself up. I wanted to watch Elise. Her arms were raised, clinging to the headboard. She was open before me. The blood pounding in my ears, drowned out the sounds we made. She sensed my gaze and opened her eyes to meet it. We did not slow down, only my perception did. In the midst of chaos of motion, sound and emotion, I found serenity.

"I shouldn't have finished inside you." I was wiping the blood from my back, sitting on the side of the bed. Elise laid still behind me, "Fills better...I don't want you to pull out." She offered nothing more. I turned to look at her, but she was staring at the ceiling. I believed she understood my concern, I wanted her to address it. "We don't need to get you pregnant." There was no answer till it was obvious that I was determined to get one. Finally, "You're really worried about knocking me up?" Elise spoke with a half-smile. She offered no biological reason that it couldn't happen. We were discussing the difference in our mentalities. I didn't want to go over the details we were both very aware of. She finally looked at me, showing a dislike for the topic. "You can't stop yourself, can you? All the things that have happened to you and you can't stop thinking about survival....Even when it's obviously hopeless." Elise put her hand up to stop us from both talking. I could see she was struggling with her thoughts. Elise put her hand on my arm as her face softened. "Ben, we don't know how much time we have. Maybe a couple of days, but maybe it's only hours....I'm glad I'm here with you....I don't want to waste our time with things we can't help." She crawled up and kissed me. Elise was initiating sex to end the conversation. I complied, but my mind was consumed.

The Agency believed in being informed. They were known to favor hidden microphones and cameras. I had assumed that the hotel had been bugged, but , when we arrived, I didn't expect to have anything that could interest them. I could find no sign of surveillance, in our little cabin. This was the hideaway for the executives. They might not have wanted their secrets to be vulnerable. We seemed to be the only residents of the resort. The Elite were most likely in hiding after the hotel attack. This could serve Elise and me. The attention elsewhere would help us go unnoticed.

Whether we were being listened to or not, I took Elise on a boat ride to ensure our privacy. Towards the middle of the lake, I stopped rowing. Elise was rubbing some areas of her body that were sore and bruised. She noticed my eyes and could anticipate my reaction, "Don't you dare apologize. I don't want you to feel bad. I want you to add to them." She added a playful wink, to set the tone. I found myself smiling, but needed to change the subject. A quick sweep confirmed we were alone on the lake. "How can you have no family, nowhere to go?" Her face sunk. Elise remained uninterested in the subject. I pressed on, "This is important, I need to know." Surrendering, Elise began to speak. "Technically, I have family, just none that will be willing to act like it right now...." My silent stare pressed her for more information. "My father..." This was difficult for her to say, "My father wasn't a good man.... He made many enemies, and he deserved their hatred...When my mom left, or was kicked out, she told me that I was God's punishment to my dad. He had been selfish his whole life, and now he would finally have to care, because he had someone he loved. Someone he knew, would pay for his sins.... People were scared of my dad, nobody had any loyalty to him.... Some people would like to watch me suffer, cause it's the closest thing to hurting my dad. Everybody else, is just too busy trying to stay alive themselves, to have any time to do anything for me....." This was not a new realization. She handled it as if it was an event that had been expected for some time. "So what can you do?" My question broke her haze. Elise's eyes shot back up at me. With a cold expression, she warned "Neither of us wants to think about that." Though we had taken very different paths, we now shared the same world. It was a bleak one.

"How are things outside the city now?"

The question caught Elise off guard. Then she was quiet as she processed it. Her mind was working, as she tried to read me at the same time. As Elise confirmed to herself my meaning, a gleam of excitement shown in her eyes. Elise's following statement proved that I had not introduced a new idea to her. She glanced around us, doing her own security sweep now. Then leaning in, she began to speak softly: "I have some reliable information, that came from my dad, and some from other people, that I'm not sure about..... Everyone agrees that the Agency doesn't have full control of the city, but they can find anyone they want inside of it. If you want to get away from them, you have to get out to the country. Now, if you're somebody they want, they have teams that specialize in finding those who get past the city limits...Unless, you go north. That's where the desert is. They say it's so dangerous, they're willing to assume you're dead if you head that way." It was all plausible. I knew that desert. It was where my father died. Chemical weapons had been used to help put down the resistance. The water and earth had been left poisoned. The "budget cuts" that Saunders had described, would have made it logical to let the barren land act as a natural barrier.

Barriers weren't needed to keep most people inside the city. As dangerous as it was, outside the A zones, the areas beyond the city limits, were much worse. I knew that wouldn't have changed while I was asleep. Checkpoints and security patrols were more about maintaining control over what came in from the outside. Only those trying to escape the agency, would risk leaving the city.

Elise and I had a connection. One that we were both still coming to grips with. We had both come to the same conclusion. However, it was desperate, nearly hopeless, course. The worst thing a rental could do, is break their contract. The "lease" was the asset that the entire economy ran on. It literally powered the machine that kept order. "Skipping out" on that lease, was a danger to civilization itself. The act was treated as such. The Agency may have been showing some signs of weakness, but the two of us were still no match for the strength it had left. This is why Elise could seem ready to surrender at one moment, and then be excited by the possibility of escape the next. This had been on her mind the whole time. There just wasn't much hope in it. Many would consider a certain, quick death, a better option than heading into that desert. And our chances were grim to even make it that far.

It was concern for me, which lead her to question my resolve. "You do know what they will do to you, if they catch you running?" I didn't want to spend much time on this: "nothing much worse than what they will do to me, if I don't." I choose to dismiss her next question, as she drew in the breath to ask it. With a shake of my head, I offered: "My mother has been dead for years, there's nothing I can do to save the woman I knew." Elise quietly nodded. We took a moment to read the commitment in each other. When satisfied, adrenaline pushed our conversation:

"We need supplies: weapons, food, and water. I'm sure we can't go to an Agency store for all we need."

"We'll have to get them from the city."

"After fifteen years, I don't know where to go."

"I think I know who can tell us."

"Who?"

"My dad's contact in outside security."

"Agency security?"

"He's more of a sub-contractor than an agent. Yes, if he thinks we're running, we're dead. But if he doesn't suspect something that serious, he's more interested in getting paid than most Agency rules."

"I've got just under 2500 left."

"That's in your Agency account. We need hard currency in the city. But if you pull more than a few hundred out, too many red flags will be sent up. It would take a miracle for us to make it out of a bank, but we would never get through an A zone gate."

"One of your father's ideas?"

"Yeah, but he had also started preparing for something like this. I know where he buried some money."

"Enough for what we need?"

"...I don't know, but I doubt it."

"We'll supplement from my account the best we can, then... negotiate well for the rest."

It was barely a plan, but there was no need more. We couldn't know what we were walking into. Details were a waste of time. The only thing I was confident about, was that it was time to leave. I had our I.D.'s in my pocket, so there was no reason to even stop in at our cabin again. We walked with purpose as we headed for the shop down from the bungalows. For some reason, I didn't feel any eyes upon me. Perhaps having a goal had eased my paranoia. Then again, perhaps we had finally bored those watching us, into leaving us alone.

Another former bomb shelter, the clothing shop was more of a high end boutique that specialized in hiking and camping apparel and gear. Activities I had been forced into as a child for survival, had been become a fashionable pastime for the wealthy. This was fortunate for us. Our preparations for escape could be disguised as an attempt to live out of our class. Most items were far too flashy for our purposes. We managed to piece together two muted outfits that would serve us well in a desert, and dark coats that would help us blend in at night. I had to resist stocking up as much as I wanted. I could not think of a good reason for carrying a tent out into the city. More than a few bottles of water and prepackaged granola bars, would raise too much suspicion. We settled for what looked natural to take for a day on the trail. Along with the water and snack bars, I purchased an emergency light, all-in-one camping knife, fishing line and hooks, and a pair of flint rocks. Matches were absent from the items for sale. Everything was overpriced. But at least we had been able to acquire some of what we needed with my account.

Elise's father had spent his last month afraid. What had motivated his fear, could only be guessed at. Elise only knew what she had confessed to him, and that his name had come up in gang chatter. He had not shared much else with his daughter. Perhaps that was all there was. Perhaps it was an attempt to shield her from danger. Perhaps it was an attempt to shield her from the knowledge that he couldn't protect her. She knew he was beginning to acquire cash and weapons. However, most of what Elise was aware of, was stored in their apartment. This was a flawed strategy. Upon any incident, agency reps would move in. Anything on their property was unless to us now. An Agency executive would have known this well. He must not have had a plan. There was only one place, which Elise knew of, where there was money we had a chance to retrieve. It was a can stuffed with paper money, on the hotel grounds. It was dangerous for us to go back there, but we had no choice.

Nothing brings calm more than surrender, but nothing brings anxiety more than hope. We waited for the sun to go down a short distance from the hotel. We could hear the activity that was still taking place on the grounds. There was dense grouping of trees that provided us with some cover. I watched Elise pace back and forth, as I leaned against a tree truck. She fidgeted with the cap from her water bottle in between drinks. This repeated as she was making laps in our little timber circle. Finally, I had to address it: "You're gonna drink all the water before we even make it out of the valley." Elise stopped and looked down at the bottle. With a sigh she closed the bottle and stuffed it back in her jacket pocket. "Sorry, I'm just..." I finished her thought: "Nervous?" "Yeah, sorry..." With a half-smile, she added: "Guess, I'm not much of a partner in crime." I returned her grin, but after a moment her attempt at a smile faded. A hint of stress took its place. I searched for the right words that would sooth her. But instead of what I was searching for, another thought struck me. It was a realization that had me feeling fear for the first time since I awoke. The thought spilled out of me awkwardly. "Elise, anyone with a rental that breaks a lease, is considered as guilty as the rental. Right now, no one has a reason to stop you from leaving. There's no law against you taking off by yourself.... You're in more danger with me." Elise found direction again, before I stopped speaking. She closed the distance between us. "Maybe more danger from the agency, but you're my only real chance.... My

Dad made sure I knew what would have happened to me, if I had been dumb enough to leave the A zones. Healthy young women, with good skin, who don't have anyone they can trust, don't fair very well out there ....He even showed me pictures of remains....You're the only hope I have." Honestly flavored her words. I reached out and took her hand. I had never been good with comforting words, but I tried. "Then we stick together, till the end." Elise wanted to speak, but the words fought her. Finally, she seized both sides of my head and kissed me hard. Pulling back she found some words: " I need to relax, and we have another hour or so before dark...Let's fuck."

The temperature dropped rapidly as the sun went down. Our breath turned to steam as we approached our former lodgings. There was still much activity on the hotel grounds. The sound of work, provided a background song for us. The land showed the wear of recent heavy foot traffic. A concern hit me, that perhaps, our treasure had already been discovered. Elise moved at a quick pace. I strained to keep up with her, while maintaining an awareness of our surrounding. The cold seemed to have pushed most of those, working the scene, up near the battered building. Elise stopped suddenly. She stood up straight, looking around. The pause gave me a moment to notice the path we had traveled. We had moved around randomly, crossed the same areas more than once. She was having trouble remembering where the stash was. She shot a scared look back at me. Her confusion was clear, as she began to open her mouth. I held a finger to my lips to silence her. Then I held my hands out flat, pushing down towards the ground, to signal her to calm down. The frustration was evident in her breathing. She looked at me in angst for a moment. I did my best to remain stoic. We were in danger. It would be very difficult to explain away our presence here. We had been warned to not come back. Sneaking back in the dark, would be more than enough reason to detain us both. Our escape would be stopped, before it even began. Elise rubbed her eyes, then spotted something to her left.

She had not seen the movement to our right. I had noticed the man just in time to act. I caught Elise, just before she was out of reach. I forced us down to our knees. Instinctively, I had covered her mouth with my hand. It muffled the protests, she tried to make. I turned her head, so that she could see him. We were lucky, he had been rubbing his ears, to warm them. The motion had made him deaf to us. His back was turned. He took his hand away from his ears. Scanning the opposite horizon, he would be able to hear us now. We were exposed. All he had to do was turn around. The rifle hung lazily over his shoulder. Elise pulled against me, but I held her still. There was too much underbrush beneath us. The sound would draw the guard's attention. He was twenty to thirty full strides away. I pulled a hand off of Elise and moved it towards the knife in my pocket. He stopped breathing on his hands, to tap himself on the forehead. He was remembering something. Searching into his jacket, he pulled out a cloth cap. He rolled it in his hands. I had seconds to make a choice. He would be deaf again for a few seconds, while rolling it over his ears. Do I charge or try to escape. My time was up, the hat was going on. I pulled Elise off the ground and set out for the nearest tree. Sinking behind a bush, my view shot back towards the guard. His cap came to a rest with our last foot step. We had not been silent. He turned in our direction. He lingered for a moment, scanning into the area we hid. His body language never showing much concern. He then began the process of smoking. It would be his main activity as he lingered.

I wouldn't describe the sentinel as vigilant, but he was awake and he was there. He meandered around in our vicinity for some time. He was more focused on sneaking swigs from his flask than observing his surroundings, but his presence kept us in our place. I could see how the waiting was affecting Elise. She wore the pain on her face. Time did seem to have slowed down. Finally, a call from near the hotel. Our company, reluctantly , strolled off in that direction. I scanned into the darkness, searching for anyone else who could surprise us. Once satisfied, I let out a muffled: "Ok, let's go," to Elise. Once again, I had to catch her. She was heading off in the wrong direction. Her intent was to escape, but I couldn't let her. "What are you doing? We have to get out of here before he comes back" she protested. I signaled her to lower her voice then spelled out my point. "We have to get what we came here for. You saw something earlier. What was it?" Elise frowned at my reasoning, but her silence showed that she agreed. She wiped her eyes, then sat up looked around. Pointing, she offered: "I think it's that tree over there." We crawled more than we walked. I gave Elise the knife to help dig, as I took look-out. It took only a minute or two for her to unearth our prize. "Can we go now?" I didn't need to answer. I took her by the hand and we made our way out into the darkness.

I tossed the knife in a trash can near the train station. How could have forgotten about the metal detectors? My mind had not been right on my previous trip here. Made of solid steel, the knife was an item that was designed to be unable to pass through valley security. All of this should have been obvious to me. I was now concerned about what else I had missed since being awake. I began to run through everything I had seen of my trip into the city, as I made my way back to Elise. The first train of the morning would not depart for more than an hour. There was a bench at the edge of the forest, within sight of the station. It was a good place for us to rest. There was a strong chance that this would be the last chance to rest, we would ever get. We were both deep in thought as I sat down next to Elise.

"I almost fucked things up last night, didn't I?" Elise's sudden statement broke my concentration. I showed her a confused look, but I knew what she was referring to. "Don't bullshit me. I almost got us caught. I know you're thinking about it." I was glad that I could honestly deny her. "That's not what I was thinking about, but, yes, we can't afford too many mistakes like last night." I raced to find to put a positive spin on my statement. "Everybody gets nervous the first time they do something like that, the next time you'll be more relaxed."

Elise shook her head. "A couple of days ago, I was shot at and nearly blown up...That should have had me more ready for sneaking around the woods last night." I disagreed: "Waiting to be shot at is much scarier that actually being shot at. If you over analyze it, it'll make thing worse. It's over; you know what your mistakes were, just try not to repeat them." Fortunately, Elise was not someone who needed an expert therapist. She just needed to hear things told to her straight. After a moment, she had a question. "What if that guard had noticed us? What would we have done?" "Kill him...and hope no one heard us doing it." It was the answer she was expecting, but not one she had come to grips with. "Not knock him..." I interrupted her before she could continue. "We have no choice but kill someone in that situation. We can't hesitate. Right now, everyone except for you and me, is our enemy. Everyone else represents death for us. The best thing for us, is to go unnoticed. We're better off not hurting anyone, but if we even think that someone is a threat...we have to deal with it."

****

CHAPTER 3

I could feel the impact, through his body, in my back. He let out a yelp as his grip loosened. I had some space to move now. I powered my head back. His nose collapsed under my skull. I was free. Spinning around, I threw my elbow out where I expected his jaw to be. I came around as Elise buried the spear back into him. He collapsed to the floor. She swung at him again, before he landed. A muffled, grown rose up behind Elise. She turned and plunged the shard of wood, back into the vendor. Elise rose back to her feet, blood dripping from the broken broom handle. Her eyes wide, breathing heavy, she scanned back and forth between each fallen man. She had saved us. Wild, Elise looked up at me, "What now?" I shook off my awe, and went to work. I picked up the vendor's knife. Searching their pockets, I found only a few valuables. I found us better camouflage, in the tattered garments hanging around us. I flung a long coat over Elise's shoulders and tore her weapon from her hands. I found a wide brimmed hat and old military coat for me. I took Elise by the hand and pulled her back the way we had been brought. Emerging back into the busy street, we seemed to capture no one's attention. Hopefully these dingy clothes would make us appear less of a target.

We had been outside the A zones for barely an hour, and we had already been attached. There had been no incidents in leaving the valley. We stopped by a banking kiosk, and withdrew 350 from my account. In an effort to avoid being noticed we decided to skip the A zone gates. Instead we made our way over the wall, at my mother's apartment building. I considered stopping in to see her, but it just didn't feel right. A janitor's closest was open on the way to the courtyard. I noticed the broken mop handle, and gave it to Elise. I rubbed grease onto our coats, hoping it would keep us from standing out. I borrowed some sheets from the laundry and fashioned them into a crude rope. We stood a bench against the wall to make it a ladder. Attached the sheets and crawled over the wall. The last hours of darkness are the quietest in the slums. Our repelling down the wall seemed to go unnoticed. Once on the ground, I realized there was no way to hide the evidence of our escape. Another mistake I had made. I tossed the rope back over wall, and wondered how many more of my errors we could survive.

Elise had met her father's contact before, but she had had no real dealings with him. She knew his name and an intersection of two streets, her father had said he frequented. As daylight broke, we found the crossway crowded with people and shops. Out of desperation, we approached the first person who was willing to speak to us. The vendor seemed to recognize the name: " T. Mason." He acted suspicious of our interest in him. It seemed to take some convincing that we had business with Mason. After some prodding, the vendor led us back into the building behind him. We followed him through narrow, dark hallways.

After the third corner, my instincts woke up. I called out to Elise. She turned, but he had the knife at her throat before she could move. The vendor wrapped his free hand over Elise's eyes and led her backwards with him. I maintained my distance, as he threatened me with the knife below her chin. We moved slowly in unison. I fixated on the position of the blade and his eyes. We were in trouble. I had to make a move. I was desperate for an opportunity. I was too focused on Elise. The other seized me from behind and soon as we entered the room. He seemed to be a foot taller than me. His arms were underneath mine, and his hands were behind my head. He lifted me into air. My struggles, only managed to turn him around. The fight was lost, until Elise struck.

A street over from the intersection was a building that rented rooms by the hour. Meant for prostitutes, it was the perfect place to take a girl, wrapped in dirty clothes, who looked in shock. No one seemed to care that I was paying for five hours to be alone with a quivering young woman, staring aimlessly at her feet. The bottle of grain alcohol was more than the room, but it was safer to wash her with than the soap and water for sale. Inside the room, I kicked, what was used as, the mattress off the frame and set Elise down on the flat cords beneath. I took the rag off her hand and began to scrub the blood off with the moonshine.

"We don't have time for this...We need to find Mason..." It was the first thing she had said since we left the bodies. Elise wasn't shaking as much by this point, but her eyes were still glazed over. There was no emotion in her voice. She looked at me with a stone face. "I'm fine," she continued. I didn't believe her. "We have enough time for you to rest....and gather yourself." "I'm gathered, we need to get moving." There was more life in this statement. I came back with, "It's okay to be upset." The haze lifted from Elise's face, "I don't need to cry about it, do you?...I didn't fuck up this time, I took care of it." She meant to be defiant, but I read some confusion in her eyes. I also felt the sting of how I interpreted her statement. "You did really good...much better than me. You saved us." I offered. Then I clarified with: "Killing those men the other night didn't phase me at all. But I'm still bothered by the first man I killed. He came after my mom, so I cut his face off with a broken bottle...I've never regretted it for a second, but I've never been okay with it either." Elise did not protest anymore. She did not cry either.

I woke up startled. I was shocked that I had been asleep. The door to our room was being pounded on. "Five minutes, or pay now!" came along with the racket. "We'll be out in four minutes!" I offered to end the disturbance. Elise seems as disoriented as I was. I had not intended to sleep. Exhaustion must have set in once I came off the adrenaline. The rest was needed, but it amounted to maybe fours of sleep in the last twenty-four. Elise rubbed her red eyes. They must have been burning like mine. Fatigue was building. Danger was increasing. "Are you ready?" Elise nodded yes, and we were gone.

We had to return to the crossway. If the bodies we had left had been found, there was no sign of it. There was no increased activity outside the building. There was a bar across the street, from where we had met the vendor. As soon as we entered the open doorway, Elise reacted to what she saw in the rear.

I had never seen Mason, but I recognized him instantly. I knew his type. The bar was crowded. Only inches separated individual bodies. That is, except for Mason's table. His back against the wall, he sat alone at a table for four. Mason stood out amongst the crowd in others ways. Sweaty and dusty, he wasn't clean, but his dirt was fresh. He lacked the aged on grime of the other bar patrons. His cigarette looked manufactured, not hand rolled. The bottle that sat of the table appeared to be a quality usually only found in the valley. It was obvious that neither had been purchased at this hole in the wall. Mason wasn't a customer of the bar. He was doing business. Mason flaunted wealth, but he wasn't a target. There was no, apparent, bodyguards, the space was given out of respect. Mason was a broker. He was not a man who took action, but he was a man who could get others to take action. His value came from his connections and knowledge. He knew what assets existed in the slums, and who possessed them. He knew what services could be provided and who provided them. Most importantly, Mason knew how to deal with these people, and what motivated them.

Elise headed for Mason as soon as soon as she spotted him. He was alert. Constantly scanning his surroundings, he noticed us weaving our way through the crowd towards him. His expression revealed that he found Elise familiar, but it took him a moment to place her. By the time we made it to his table, Mason had a smile of recognition. He motioned for us to sit down. I wanted to remain standing. We were already too vulnerable, but I knew that it wasn't really an optional request. Mason didn't speak till we were seated. It was loud in the bar, but he choose to keep his volume moderate. Speaking below the level of the ambient sound did provide a measure of privacy, but this was not his only motivation. It was all part of his method. It established his control. We had to lean in to hear him clearly. Leaving us even more exposed in unfamiliar surroundings. He focused on Elise:

"You've grown up."

"You recognized me that quick?"

"Same pretty face you had as a little girl...That body sure has spouted out into a sexy woman."

Elise's outfit was far from form fitting, but this was part of his method too. Objectifying her so blatantly, so quickly, was meant to drive home that he was in power. Establishing that her worth was measured only by what she had to offer him.

"My condolences about you father. I may be the only other person, besides you, that is actually sorry he's dead....I'll miss the steady income."

Elise powered through the second insult.

"I need your help."

Mason held up his hand to stop Elise's speech.

"Let's not use the word help...Help is for work that is done for free...I don't work for free. "

All his efforts to establish the rules of the game, were a good sign. Believing us to be novices, would leave him less suspicious of our activities.

"Then we need to buy information from you"

Mason smiled wryly. "I'm not cheap, do you think you can afford it?"

"We're looking for a party.. I mean, we need to know who throws the best parties.."

"You planning to do a lot of partying?"

Elise's answer was delivered with the perfect amount of awkwardness and shame.

"He's looking to party now...I'm gonna need to know who puts on the best parties..after he goes back to sleep..."

We couldn't ask him where we could buy guns and supplies for the desert. Mason would have turned us into the Agency immediately. We needed a cover story, and Elise came up with a brilliant one. If we just asked for girls and drugs, we might get sent to a low level pimp. That would be a dead end for our needs. We needed a big operation. We were looking for a dealer that had clientele rich enough to afford to what it cost to spend the night with a woman of Elise's class. It was obvious that Mason understood what Elise meant, but he offered nothing but a poker face for a moment.

"Usually takes a little longer than this for girls like you to end up this desperate."

".... My Dad left me nothing. No one else will help me....If it wasn't for Ben, I wouldn't have anywhere to sleep or anything to eat the last couple of days..."

Mason studied her for another moment.

"I can put you with the best outfit, but my referral fee isn't cheap. Of course, that doesn't have to be paid in cash. Since you're looking to start that kind of work, I have use of a room upstairs?"

"Fuck No!" The words erupted out of me. Too much of my honesty came through. Mason showed suspicion of my reaction. I moved to cover my mistake. "I don't know where you've been, and I'm going in her raw. I've got to use condoms with the other whores, but I wanna feel something with at least one of these bitches...." I lowered the intensity of my voice, as I moved to establish that I had no real affection for Elise. " You fuck her all you want, when I'm back asleep, but I don't wanna risk catching any flesh rot you might have..... I want to have a chance of my dick working when I wake up 20 years from now." Mason was offended. It was dangerous to piss him off, but safer to have him angry than suspicious. The smart move would have been to send Elise up to the room with him. I did not consider that an option. I shot Mason my best poker face. Our cover was that I was a rental looking for a party. I wouldn't need him to find a party. He started to smile, but his eyes were still pissed. "Well, cash, it is... " He stamped at his cigarette. It was a stall while he thought about numbers. "Referral fee is.. 650." His offer was disrespectful. Without respect, we just became an easy target for him. I had to give him a reason to believe we weren't an easy Mark. I pulled away from the table. "Do you think I'm that stupid, or just that desperate?... I'm not paying that, just to know where to get our shit at!" Without missing a beat "Well, you want to know who has the girls without the flesh rot, right?..." I didn't want to play it too calm. I gave him a little crazy, hoping to back him off. "I'm not some executive's kid. I grew up in the camps! I know you're just trying to fuck us. This is a clean valley girl, right here. Gangs will fight over somebody like her. You can get your money from them. Elise, let's go!" Mason went back to Elise. "Listen, you don't want to end up with some low class pimp. You want someone who realizes how valuable you can be, somebody who has the connections for you to work in the valley. You don't want to end up tied to a mattress in a tent, with a line outside!" He was selling hard. We were getting somewhere. I seized Elise by the arm. Mason clung to her other arm. "200 and I'll set you up with a high class outfit." I moved for the close. Leaning in:" She doesn't have any money." On cue, Elise turned to me and pleaded. "Please, I'll make it worth 200. Whatever you want!" I paused and tried to find my creepiest face possible. "Whatever?..." Shame and regret shined across Elise's face: "Yeah." I turned back to Mason and accepted his terms.

Mason told us to return in three hours. I didn't like having to wait. He claimed he needed the time to find the best "deal" for us. He would not budge on this. I agreed but did not plan to sit around and wait. We left the bar hoping to find another source. Our best chance was at the market. The agency patrolled the market. I didn't know if we were wanted , but I didn't want to risk their attention. However, their presence is also what made the market the safest place to be in the slums. Fortunately, the agency guards were more interested in extorting the merchants, than spending time investigating the crowd. There was no luck finding an alternative to Mason. The best we could do was invitations to do deals away from the market. Obvious set ups, to lead us into a trap.

Without any other options, we returned to Mason after the three hours. We paid our money, and got our address. I tried to read Mason. He did not appear to be pleased with the deal. You never want to your salesman happy. This could be a good sign, but he could also just be really good at the game.

There are two types of dangerous men: Stable and Unstable. They present different challenges when being dealt with. A stable man's actions can be predicted. He always does what is in his best interests. If you are a benefit to him, you are not only safe from him, he might even protect you in some cases. Pose no risk to him, and he will leave you alone. But if you are a threat, he will always strike. An unstable man does not follow any logic. His decisions are made on a whim. The emotion of the moment, is more important than the result of the action. An unstable man is a constant danger to everyone. The only time it is better to deal with an unstable man, than a stable one, is when you are an apparent risk. Sometimes they don't attack, just because they should.

The man we were brought to was unstable. He appeared to be around Elise's age. His eyes were wide and full as energy, but showed the signs of a lack of sleep. Random movement filled his body. The use of stimulants was apparent. The few years he had lived, had been hard. He sat behind a desk. Others in the group stood around the small room. What light the room had was focused on where, Elise and I had been stood. The man behind the desk was the only face I could make out clearly. He ignored Elise, he had been focused on me from the moment I came into sight. Every other man we had passed, had been much more interested in staring at the healthy attractive, valley girl I was with. His attention made me more uneasy. Being brought all the way to the back room was already a bad sign. Our business shouldn't have been that important.

It looked like a large tent from the outside. Once the curtain was peeled back, the buildings structure was visible. Canvas had been used to fill in the gaps of the old concrete and steel skeleton. We dropped Mason's name and the appointment time, he gave us, and we were lead inside. They had tried to cover the signs of the digging, but I noticed the disturbed ground. The newly constructed knee wall was a dead giveaway. Explosives were buried as a front line defense. They were most likely directional mines. This was a well-armed group. Inside the front door was a large common area. Gang members were scattered throughout. Assault weapons were displayed prominently. They were far from, on high alert. A group played cards around a table. Others encircled a woman dancing topless. Many just sat or laid on pieces of furniture, obviously high on something. They were well equipped , but not well organized. Had it not been for Elise's physical appeal, we would not have been noticed, except by those men we had met at the door. We had not been asked what we wanted. The important members of the gang should not want to expose themselves to those looking to "party" the way we had insinuated to Mason. Negotiations for drugs and girls, should have been handled up front. Heading back to the well-guarded area, I knew something was wrong.

"You don't know who I am, do you?" He seemed somewhat offended by my ignorance. My first thought was that he enjoyed seeing people afraid of him. I moved quickly to dismiss any slight he felt. "I've been asleep for fifteen years. Everything has changed out here. " His face softened. A chaotic, awkward laugh was belted out. "I was just a little shit back then!" He face snapped back to serious. With a demanding tone, he delivered: "You remember Constance Williams?" The surprise must have been evident on my face. "Mrs. Williams?" When he spoke the name "Williams", I looked at his face for more than just an attempt to read his intentions. I saw the eyes and nose that I had seen so many years before. Only they had been on his mother. It was the younger son, Jimmy, that had shared these with her. "You're Jimmy?" He seemed to enjoy when I recognized her name, but not when I spoke his. Suddenly his hand was in the air, grasping a gun. It was more pointed in my direction, than aimed at me. He moved it as he spoke. It was like a prop that he used to talk with his hands. "Did I say you could call me Jimmy? My mom and my brother, were the only ones, who could call me Jimmy!" I raised my hands in surrender. "I'm sorry, I meant no disrespect! That's just what I knew you as..." He froze for a moment, his expression changed and the armed hand fell to the desk. "Yeah, you're right." The awkward smile returned. "Fuck...You go ahead and call me "Jimmy," I mean, you're basically family....Maybe all that I have." I was afraid to touch the subject, but it seemed liked he wanted me to ask. "So, is your Mom and brother?" Jimmy shook his head yes: "Mom went nine years ago...Bobby....last year." It was difficult for him to speak of his brother. He might have dealt with his mother's loss, but his brother was still fresh for him. "I'm sorry," was the best I could offer. "Shit happens," was his quick response, as he began to noticeably shake more. "So yeah, you might be the closest thing to family I have left." He repeated the observation. It must have been strong on his mind, or he wanted it on my mind.

"It's a good thing Mason used your whole name, when he was looking for a deal.... Shouldn't trusted him... He said you were looking for a party, but he was looking for the highest bidder for both your asses....... Said he had a valley girl that would be good for pimpin out, and a rental named "Ben Darbold."....... Said you'd have some cash on you and two good "A" zone I.D.'s. Said he wanted the rental treated badly, but we had to leave you breathing and with brain function. As long as you're alive and your brain works, you can be hooked up back to the sleep machines." I wasn't surprised to hear of Mason's betrayal, but I wasn't sure if Jimmy offering the information was good or bad.

I responded with: "I didn't like him, but we were desperate." It was obvious we were vulnerable, there was nothing to gain by trying to hide it. "Desperate for a party?" Jimmy may have been high and sleep deprived, but he could tell I wouldn't have put myself in this position just to have a little fun. I would need a more plausible story. "I need guns." I offered it boldly. Jimmy was unsurprised. "Why does a rental on leave, need guns?" " There's some thugs shaking down my mom. I need to wipe them out before I go under again. " It was the best story I could come up with. For the first time, Jimmy demeanor was constant and quiet. "We can't send guns inside the A zone!" It was the first time someone from the gang, besides Jimmy, had spoken. Jimmy's spun to face the figure. His voice was set afire with: "Did anybody fucking ask you!" The boss was handling business, and the man had shown disrespect by speaking out of turn. Jimmy's hand was white from griping his gun so tight. The man cowered. "I'm sorry Mr. Williams!" Jimmy slowly came back to face me.

"Dumbshit's got a point. Agency is looking for a excuse to kill people like us. Us giving you the guns, to go shootin up the A zone with, is more than plenty."

"No one will ever know I got the guns from you."

"Mason sent you here. Can't trust him to keep his mouth shut."

"I mean, no one will find out I did it. The Agency would never give me another leave if they knew. I'm gonna take them out and get rid of all the evidence. "

"How do you know that's all it is? How do you know they don't have friends? How do you know they're not my friends?"

"These guys are small time. The racket they're working isn't really worth the time they're spending. These old people don't have anything to take. You've got a real high class operation here. Not worth the trouble of crossing into the A zone, to shake down some retirees."

Mr. Williams rubbed his face with his unarmed hand. Jimmy was thinking hard. I had answered the questions as best I could. So far, I had managed to not leave any, glaring, holes. I was hoping he didn't ask why I brought Elise with me here. I could not come up with anything plausible. Honestly, I was wondering why I had done it, at that moment. He stood up and came around the desk. Jimmy's face was close to mine. He was sizing me up. "How many times did you fuck my mom?" The question stunned me. His stare was intent on my face. My cover relaxed as I was caught off guard. My answer was not part of a plan. I told the truth, because I didn't know what else to do. "We were together once." Jimmy reacted like he was expecting it to have happened more. Prepared anger began to seep into face, as he question my number. "Only one time?" "Yes." He pulled back some. "What, was she not worth the extra food, it cost, another time? Did ya find someone hotter, to get drunk the other times? Or was she only dumb enough, to get caught alone with you, more than once?" It had went bad. Jimmy had made his mind up before I walked through the door. He was looking to settle, what he thought, was an old score. I began to count the men in the room with us. I tried to make eye contact with Jimmy while I appraised my chances of getting his gun from him. I also found myself angry. I was offended by his insinuations. "It wasn't like that." Jimmy stopped. I had his attention. "I was scared kid. Nothing would have happened if she hadn't wanted it to." He approached me again. I prepared to make a move. His face returned to a vague, awkward, expression. "You know, I don't really remember you. Your face looks like I've seen it before, but I wouldn't been able to place it.... She just talked about you so much." Pain took over his face. He had not came to grips with his mother's death. He backed off and began to pace about the room. "There were a whole lotta men, that I heard about. You were the only one she ever smiled when talking about." He was fighting to retain control of himself. "She always said that she hoped me and Bobby, turned out like you...Bobby just said that she was hintin, that we should rent ourselves out. So she could get a nice, A zone, apartment like your mom..." He looked crazed. There was a battle inside his head. "You're saying that you did all that stuff for us, just out of the goodness of your heart, and mom just put out cause she needed to get laid?" Bitter sarcasm filled his words.

I needed him to get close to make my move, and challenging him was the best way to accomplish that. But that wasn't the reason for my tone. I was mad. I was tired of playing the games. I had lived with fear my whole life. I had sold fifteen years, hoping to end some of the fear. But I had awoken scared. I was afraid that I would discover, just what I would go on to discover. I was done being afraid. If it ended here, then Elise and I would go out fighting. They had not checked us for weapons. Elise had her blade and she had shown she could use it. If I could get Jimmy's gun, we had a little chance. It was better for us to die quick, than live to suffer their abuse. Whatever happened, Mr. Williams was about to hear the truth. " Our group stuck together like a family! We helped each other! I never asked your mother to earn anything. Why she wanted sex that day, I don't know. But I was a young man, and she was a beautiful woman, so I did it!" "But you showed us that we weren't really you're family, when you left us!" It wasn't sex with his mother that had Jimmy upset. The stories his mother had told him, had given him the impression, that life would have been better if I had stayed in the camps. He didn't remember me being around. There was no real knowledge that would take away from the fantasy that he had built in his head. His mother had become so bitter, that simply not hating me, had made me the best candidate for a father he ever knew of. Jimmy was acting as an abandoned son. I had to answer for all the wrongs that had ever been done to him. "I didn't abandon you!" I had his attention. The emotion began to color my voice. "I couldn't protect anyone in the camps. I was too outnumbered... I sold myself, hoping, that I would be able to protect some of those, I cared about...I gave my life up so that my sister and mother could have one...Only, I wake up to find that my sister had to sell herself too, because I failed....Now, I just want a chance to save what little I have left..."

Jimmy stared at me for a moment. He had an expression that I had not seen before. It was an awkward silence. No one in the room, knew what to do. We all stood frozen. Finally........ he moved. He motioned to follow with a quick, "C'mon." Jimmy lead us back to the front room, and then over to its side. Behind a locked, heavy door, we came to a caged in, room. It was an arsenal. Jimmy keyed in, the code, to the pad lock, and we went inside. Assault rifles, body armor, explosives, and rocket launchers all hung on the ways. I had been through a war, but this was the best stocked weapons depot, I had ever seen. Jimmy turned to me, and in a low voice: "you're runnin, right?" I'm not sure why, but I told the truth. "Yeah." "Good, that's smart." He turned and opened a cabinet full of small arms. Two revolvers, a .45 and a 9mm were produced. "Auto's are no good for you. Best to head into the desert, too hard to keep the sand out. Plus, hard to get good bullets once you leave the city. Automatic will jam up too much. Get a bad round in one of these, and just pull the trigger again, move on to the next hole." Then he handed us a box of ammunition for each. Next, there was a sawed off, double barrel shotgun, and a belt with ten extra rounds on it. "Same thing with the scatter gun, this'll fire shit made in a cave." Jimmy searched around till he found a box under a countertop. "This is a crossbow kit. Put it together when you get out of the city. It'll be good for huntin stuff. It's pretty quiet, and you can make more arrows, if you need." Elise and I began to hide our new weapons inside our clothes. Jimmy sat a backpack down in front of me. "This is what the Agency sends with their people, when they go into the desert. It's full of survival shit. A tent, dried food, and stuff for water. There's things that get water out of the air, and stuff that cleans water. I think you can even make your own piss clean." "We don't have much money." Jimmy just shook his head, and did not acknowledge my statement. " Head straight north into the desert, at least, a couple of miles. Then go east. There's a town five miles, straight over from here. That's where people get fucked up, don't go there. Agency is all over that place. Go ten more miles through the desert, before you turn back south. There's a few villages out there. The Agency can't afford to keep people out that far anymore, but most people out there will still trade for your Agency cash. After that, you've got to figure it out for yourself." For the first time that day, Jimmy did not want to look at me. I wanted to say something to him, but I was having a hard time coming out of fight or flight. It was an awkward moment. Jimmy waived his hand in front of him "Get the fuck outta here, before I get smart."

"AGENCY! IT'S A FUCKING RAID!" The announcement set off a flurry of activity. Jimmy pushed by us, as he raced to the front room. Lethargic members of the gang, came alive. A loud speaker, bellowed outside. "This is an official inspection. Prepare to be..."

There is an art to explosives. Beyond constructing the devices, there is a feel for how to place them, and when to set them off. They did not go off at once. Smaller charges, buried outside the entrance, began to pop. Their force brought down some of the canvas sheeting that made up the front wall. It gave a good view of the soldiers, being torn apart by the shrapnel. Their riot gear failing to protect them, as the blasts rose up from their feet. The lights, from the armored vehicle, were blinding as it charged. I knew what was coming next. I tried to get between it and Elise. I knew about directional bombs. I knew how difficult it was to actually control a large explosion. I knew none of these men were, enough of an artist, to do so. The earth erupted. Reality shook, as a wall of air crashed through us. Those racing towards the chaos, found themselves hanging, suspended above the ground. Bits of concrete, rock, and metal, became missiles, tearing off skin and flesh. Elise and I impacted the ground, on our backs. Deaf and dizzy, we fought our way to our feet. Elise's ears, must have been ringing as loud as mine. I was shouting instructions to her, but she couldn't have been able to hear. I didn't need to tell her to get the guns. She was already pulling compact machine guns and ammo off the walls. I seized upon the body armor, I had spotted when we entered the room. Drugs and adrenaline can help a person hard to stop. Despite the explosion, many in the gang, still had fight in them. The shock wave had pulled the boxes away from a heavy machine gun sitting in the middle of the front room. Jimmy brought it to life as he unleashed .50 caliber rounds randomly into the cloud of dust. Fortunately for us, someone had the foresight, to install an escape door, in the armory. There was a back door to the cage. It could only be unlocked from inside. We spilled out into a musky dark hallway. We ran wildly, carrying ourselves and our gear as fast as we could.

The loudest thing in my head, was a high-pitched squeal, but I could make the sounds of war out underneath it. Motion lamps lit up the end of the hallway, as we can to it. There was another heavy door, locked from the inside. I slid the bolt to the side, and kicked it open. We came out into an old parking garage. It had been turned into a cardboard and tent slum, by the homeless. The last of those residents were still scurrying out, as we entered. We trampled the makeshift housing, as we twisted through the maze of trash and cement columns. A wall came down behind us. Brick and mortar were airborne, as a tank plunged through. It was heavily armed, and we had nowhere to hide. Only a few yards behind us, I turned and raced for it. A hatch popped open, as a man emerged up, behind a duel machine gun mount. I leapt onto the cabin. Throwing one case onto the vehicle, I swung the other to bash the soldier in the face. He brought up his arms to block the blow. I struck him again. He was a big man. The hatch way was a tight fit for him. The only way to get to his side arm, was to push him up out of the tank further. As he ascended, I was able to knock him off balance. I seized the gun as he slide off the roof. I set the pistol to fully automatic and plunged it down into the hatch. I opened it up widely. The bulleted ricocheted off the metal interior, creating crossfire inside the tank. I peeked down, to make sure the other two members of the crew were dead. Elise had noticed my reversal, and made it back to me. I tossed our bags through the hatch, and pulled her up. She may have been trying to question my plan, but I grabbed her and shoved her into the vehicle.

The blow, to the back of my head, stunned me. I was already off, because of the explosion. The punch left my vision blurred and my equilibrium spinning. My face landed against the tank. I was able to make out the fist, coming again. I through a hand up, and was able to deflect it some. The first man out of the tank, had returned to the fight. The armored vehicle shook, and raced forward. We had been impacted by a second tank. We were sent rolling forward. The soldier and I were left lying beside each other. Suddenly, the tank stopped, be we didn't. We rolled together as a ball, on to the lower, front, of the tank, till we landed against the pillar, the tank impacted. The second armored cars guns strafed our vehicle. A shower of bullets drenched the raised back, of our tank. The engine beneath me, roared as Elise took control of it. Tires squealed, as we shot back at our attacker. Catching them at an angle, the other vehicle was spun around. The soldier manning the machine gun, was thrown from his post. The gears screamed, as Elise shifted out of reverse. We took off forward. I kicked at the soldier. He grabbed my leg, and wrestled to on top of me. I punched at his face, but his helmet and face shield, kept most of my punishment from reaching him. The tank plowed through the flimsy slum. Debris flowed over the front of the tank, and in the middle of our fight. Shot rang out again, from the second tank. Sparks from the hits, danced up the side of our tank, as Elise swerved to miss a column. The sharp turn loosened the soldier's position above me. My free hand found a wooden board. I brought this board down onto the soldier's helmet. I bounced his head between my bat and the tank. Another dramatic steering adjustment, flipped the soldier back on top of me. This time, he was dazed. I took him by the throat and tossed him off the tank. I watched him fall, then checked my hand to make sure I had pulled the pin. He was struggling to stand up, when the grenade dismembered him. The sudden cloud of smoke and flesh, caused our pursing tank to veer. It went full speed into column. When first built, the column would have withstood that force. But it was too degraded by now. The fractured concrete and rusted rebar gave way, allowing gravity to bring the ceiling above down. I watched as huge sections of the ancient garage began to collapse. Then the floor seemed to give beneath us. I sailed off the front of the tank, and continued to fall.

I don't remember my fall ending. The world was distant. I remember being held up. I remember trying to walk. I remember Elise. The ringing was so loud, my head vibrated. The world spun in one direction, and I spun the other. All light began dim, and then brightened. The intensity would become blinding, and the then all went dark. Nothing was solid. The walls moved in waves. I fell onto the ceiling. I looked up at the floor.

And then, I was awake. I was sitting up. Reality had returned. More than returned, it felt intense. My senses felt more alive than I could ever recall. Somehow, that dark and dank room was vibrant. "You're back." I turned to find a grinning Elise. "How do you feel?" I didn't need to answer the question. She knew I felt good, and that I thought it was too good. Elise shook an empty medicine vile in front of me. She had injected me with something.

"I'm High?"

"No, you're pretty much the exact opposite. This is, uhm, well it's got a really long scientific name, but called it "free pass" back in college. Basically it super charges your immune system. A shot of this and you do about a week's worth of healing an hour. We kept it around in case anyone O.D.ed.... It's really good for concussions and internal bleeding. Which, I'm sure you had at least one of those after your fall."

"Where did you...?"

"Your friend Billy had a stack of it, right next to all his ammo. It was developed for use in combat. Not much value to a junkie, it sobers you up immediately. "

An old memory came to mind:

"My dad was right...The corporations did have a super soldier drug, during the revolution."

"Yeah, they did. The problem with this stuff is, you take once and it saves your life, but if you keep taking it often, you end up with super charged cancer. Most of the soldiers dosed, that survived the revolution, were dead within a year. "

I became alarmed: "How long have I been out?"

"About two and half hours."

"Where are we?"

"Some sort of storage room, in the old subway system."

"We need to get..."

"I unloaded the armored car. All of our stuff, and everything I could pull out, is in here with us. Then I blew the opening. It closed off the tunnel in that direction too. It'll take them quite a while, to dig through all that ruble."

"We need to secure this room."

"I've got motion sensor grenades, in the direction that's still open, at fifty feet and hundred yards. Anyone gets near, and we'll know it. I've got a remote for them too. So we can turn them off when we need to exit."

My mind was racing, searching for something she had missed. Finally, I sat back down when I had come up with nothing. I realized that I was no longer Elise's protector. We were a team. "Well, you saved me once again." Her eyes lit up as she smiled. "Well, I'm also the one that crashed you through a wall in the first place." There was a pop and crackle of static. I searched for its source. Elise moved to reveal a box beside her. "I managed to rip the radio out of the tank." A voice came through it. Locations were being announced. Orders were being given out. They were in code, but I knew what the basic idea was. "They're locking down the city." Elise nodded in agreement. "They've already given the order for all valley residents, to return there. In four hours, only high level personal will be able to get in or out. All security reservists, are being called up now. The outside borders will be secured, then they'll start setting up checkpoints on the streets. By nightfall, there will be teams sweeping the buildings and...down here in the tunnels."

The Agency was spooked. Emergency protocols had been instituted. They might have been surprised by the level of fight that Billy's gang had managed to put up. Perhaps, they had become aware of our involvement. Instead of just running, they could have theorized we were leading some larger conspiracy. It was also possible, that the violence of the last few days, had the elite realizing that there power was slipping away. This mobilization was a last, desperate attempt to regain control. "Have you heard our names?" Elise shook her head no. "There hasn't been the "rental runner" code either." I was struck by her knowledge. "How do you know the runner code?" Elise sighed: "I didn't think my dad would be able to get me out of a security detail. So I started doing some studying...I had gotten really bored over the last year...We should get moving. Every minute that goes by, the harder it will be to get out." She was right. As we sat there, our opponents were organizing. But they were already organized. Our task had been close to impossible, to begin with. A situation can only get so close to impossible, before it is just that.

As Elise stood up, she rose into more of our limited light. As I watched, an urge came over me. I discovered something I wanted more than to escape. I found something I wanted more, than I had wanted anything in my life. I wanted more time with Elise. All I had to trade for it, was my last chance to avoid capture. That chance was small anyway. At that moment, I would have traded a good one. I stood up and used my hand, to her chin, to bring her eyes up to mine. "I want to be with you, once more, before we leave." I could see that she knew, what I knew. This was our last chance to be alone. Almost certainly, we would soon die running. I didn't dread this fate. I was thankful for this moment I had with Elise. There was much we would never have, but we did have something few ever get. We had the opportunity to know, we were spending our last few hours together. We could remove everything else from our minds, and focus on each other. She fell into my arms. I held her tight. I took my time enjoying the smell of her hair, as we lingered in our embrace. This would not be rushed. We pulled apart just enough to bring our lips together. I began to slowly pull off her coat. We wouldn't speak again, for some time.......

We had covered the old countertop with our clothes. We laid there together, still naked. For a while, we pondered just holding out in this room till the end. Just passing the time in each other's arms, until we made our final stand. We joked about setting a goal, for the amount of times we should have sex before we were discovered. It was appealing, but it was neither Elise's nor my nature. We were fighters, and we had to attempt to make it out.

We had too much gear to carry. We took the guns we could hide underneath our coats. We used bags, from the tank, to make back packs. Inside those we stuffed the survival supplies. We could put on the body armor as our first layer of clothing. The helmets had to be stuffed in with our food. The remote controlled grenades and a collapsible rocket launcher finished up, what we could carry. We would be hot and weighed down, but we were equipped for a spectacular fight. The monorail would be the fastest way to the city limit, but that wasn't an option for us. We still had our A zone I.D.'s, but not only would we have to shed every weapon, even the survival supplies would get us stopped. All, tossing our equipment, would buy us, was a trip back to the valley for Elise and one to Acoma for me. We would have to walk out of the city. The best chance was to use the underground, as far as we could. Then we'd try to work our way through the city ruins. Each check point was an obstacle that would have to be faced, as we came to it.

In a city where no shelter went unused, the old subway tunnel was surprising devoid of signs of occupation. The reason became clear a quarter of a mile down from our room. Our flashlights revealed a wall of debris that had sealed the tunnel. When I was young, the Agency had a difficult time controlling the underground. It was an expansive system, with many access points. As resources became limited, it would have made sense, to just close off parts of the underground. "When I blew the doorway, we made, I might have trapped us down here." There was no despair in Elise's voice. That was a benefit of accepting that you were already in a hopeless scenario. I felt no anxiety either: "Think we can get in fifty good fucks, before our supplies run out?" After my question, I began to scan the walls that we had past. Elise stood still. "Would a Yes, or a No, motivate you more to try for it?" In a way, it was comforting to not see a way out. Then, I saw the writing. Elise noticed my reaction, and joined me. It was a code. A code used by smugglers. Before I signed my lease, I tried joining a group of smugglers. There was profit in moving contraband across the zones, we had back then. Of course, the profit was due to the danger. I was still a low level grunt, when most of the group was busted. I was lucky that I had not been involved with anything enough, to be worth selling out. After the close call, I saw The Agency as a more sure way to get Jazzy and Mom out of the camps. To the untrained eye, the code blended in with the rest of the graffiti that littered the walls. I knew enough to pick it out, but not to fully translate it. It was a marking for an entrance into a secure location. When the tunnel began to rumble, I knew which location it was. We had found a secret door into a train station.

The dusty old lock was industrial grade. It would have taken welding gear to cut through it. Fortunately, Elise had rescued a lock picking kit from the tank. A push of a button, and the hand held machine, made a key that fit inside the lock. Something was blocking the door. I could get it open a crack, just enough to there was no light on the other side. Forcing my way through could cause our detection, but there was no other way. Elise and I went over the scenario. If we set off an alarm, this would be the climax. We took out our X8, sub-machine guns, they were our heaviest firepower. We put on our helmets. Elise produced a grenade from her jacket:

"If too much hell comes back at us, we blow this hole, and go with plan B."

"The 50 fucks?"

"We've got a lot of supplies. I want more than 50."

"You remember, I'm an old man, right?"

"Don't worry, I've got two more vials of that drug. I bet it can do amazing things for your dick."

"Was that the real reason you grabbed it?"

"You better hurry up, with the door, old man. Give me another minute to think about it, and I might make staying in the tunnel Plan A."

I switched the inferred sight, attached to the X8, on, and took a deep breath. All my weight went into the door. The obstruction gave way. I fell forward into a wave of falling metal. The sound of the crashing, echoed back at me. I landed hard on the scattered shelving. The scope was up to my eye, before I even rolled over. Through the green display, I found myself in a small storage room. I brought the sight to bear on the room's other doorway. The racket, I had created, would surely bring someone's attention. This could be our last stand. I stopped breathing, to get as silent as possible. I strained to catch the slightest sound of motion, coming our way. There was none. Only the subtle sound of the cans, I had split, rolling along the floor. Finally, came the sound of Elise, taking in air. She had been holding her breath too. I gathered myself, and made it to my feet. I was cautious, as I crossed the short distance to the door. The handle squeaked when I turned it. The need of a good greasing, spoke of the area's lack of maintenance. I came out onto a dim hallway. The only light source, came from twenty yards, to my right. I crept down the passageway. The light was shining through a window of a door. As we approached, a stairwell became visible on the side.

We found ourselves in the bowels of a train station. We had managed to circumvent the checkpoints, and enter back into the A zones. Two flights up the staircase, we found a restroom. We may have avoided being searched, but our appearance still presented a problem. The garbs that had allowed us to blend into the slums, would have the opposite effect on the monorail. We concocted a story of being merchants, who were trading in the market, when the violence broke out. We could claim to have cast off our better clothes, when the locals became hostile. Before my sleep, this might have been a plausible scenario. Elise did not seem confident in it. I gathered this practice had changed in the last fifteen years. We needed our coats to hide our weapons, so we had no choice. We washed as much dirt and grime from our hands, faces and hair as we could. We inspected each other for noticeable signs of armament. A quick kiss and we were off.

We emerged from the "Employees Only" area, seemingly unnoticed. The top level of the station was packed. Everyone's attention was towards the tracks. A train heading towards the Valley was passing through. The crowd was angry it wasn't stopping. The security personal were all occupied, just trying to maintain order. We were closest to tracks that lead to the valley. We needed to cross over to get to outbound traffic. Our luck seemed to be holding out, as we discovered that we were heading in the least popular direction. The crosswalk over the north bound tracks, were almost empty. We came down in between the rails. Now it was just a matter of waiting. That was the problem. With few in the outbound waiting area, we stood out.

We were noticed quickly. The guards in our area were green. It made sense. Keep your most experienced people were the crowd was. Let the rookies be where the least action was. A veteran, might not have cared about a couple heading away from the Valley, but this kid was by the book. I could tell he knew something was wrong about us. However, I could also tell he was scared. He knew he should investigate, but he was struggling to find the courage. There was nothing we could do but hope. Any attempt to leave, could empower him enough to act. We had to try to seem natural. At first he was just paying special attention to us, glancing our way more than anywhere else. Then he was staring. Our train was coming. Just a few minutes more, and we would be on our way. Not safe, but we would have one more hurdle behind us. The cars were pulling in. I checked to see if our sentinel was watching. He caught me looking his way. I could see his adrenaline from 30 feet out. The train was slowing down. Forty-five seconds, and we would be on board. He was walking towards us. The air from the brakes whistled, signaling the doors were about to open. I tried to appear casual as I pushed Elise towards, a soon to open door. "Halt! Step to the side!" Instinctively, Elise started to stop. I used my hand on her back, to keep her momentum forward. Obliviousness, was our best play. It was loud on the deck; not hearing him, was possible. Through the ambient clamor, came his footsteps. I could feel Elise being tugged in the other direction. "I said halt!"

I turned to find his young face flushed. He had managed to turn his adrenaline to anger. I tried to seem apologetic. "We're are you going?" He should have asked for our I.D.'s first. We would have no argument, for heading north, once our I.D.'s were scanned. I hoped this mistake meant we had a chance. "Home" I responded. I didn't know the name of anywhere we could live to the north. My answer exacerbated the officer. "Area 9, we live in Area 9" offered Elise. "Step to the side!" He commanded. "But the train is about to leave" I protested. He presented the assault rifle that hung on his side. "I said!...Step to the side!" "Please! We just want to go home!" Pleaded Elise. Then his anger turned to confusion. "You live in Area 9? Let me see your I.D.'s." We were busted. The monorail doors opened behind us. Elise threw up a hand towards me, as if to back me off. The guard seemed to relax as I took a step back. He was watching me, as Elise took control of his weapon. She spun it around and disemboweled him with 45 caliber shells. Ripping the gun from the falling corpse, Elise spent the rest of the clip into the air. The mass of people, became a sea of chaos. Most of the guards were overcome by the scattering flock. I ripped open my jacket, to get to my own gun, as I screamed "Train!" to Elise. She sped through the opening and made towards the front car.

I pulled my X8 mini-assault rifle, from beneath my coat. At only 15 inches in length, and made completely of carbon fiber, it was Light and small. There were three setting of fire: Semi-auto, one bullet per trigger pull, Burst, two shots per pull or two shots per second, of trigger held, and fully automatic. It fired a mid-sized rifle round that utilized an advanced plastic casing, over a metal projectile. The weight saving feature allowed us to carry a few hundred rounds. Already set on Semi-Auto, I pumped two shots into a guard to my right. Laying down suppressing fire, I retreated back into the railcar. Glancing back, I found a guard charging towards the opposing entrance. The first round caught him center mass, stopping momentum cold. The second shattered the plastic facemask, and removed the helmet, as it exited his head. Bits of plastic and fiberglass scrapped by face. My back was being fired upon. I clicked into full-auto as I spun around. Diving backwards, I held the trigger. A stream of bullets was sent into three advancing soldiers. I crashed onto the floor as the train began to lurch forward. The X8 emptied as the doors closed. Elise had managed to put the monorail into drive. Now she was racing back towards me. She screamed out "Ben!" I raised my hand to show her I was alive. Bullets ripped through the wall beside Elise. She did not attempt to take cover. Her response was a hail of her gunfire back at her attackers. I popped in a new clip and joined her assault. The tram came up to speed slowly.

Through the windows, I could see soldiers boarding the rear of the train. I dropped my backpack, took out my helmet, and took off to the rear. If we let them organize and advance, they would have the advantage. The passenger cars did not provide a good position to defend, and in the front, we would have nowhere to retreat. My coat was heavy and awkward, but I had to keep it on. If I dropped it, I might not have a chance to go back for it. We needed to keep as many of our supplies on us, as possible. I flung open the door, between cars, and rushed through. I was fighting to reload the gun, while keeping my speed up. The clip clicked in as my jacket caught on to a bench. Hoping on one foot, I struggled to maintain my balance, as momentum carried me forward. The sudden movement dropped, the unsecured helmet, off my head. I caught it with my left hand as I steadied myself back into a full gallop. The side of the helmet was used as a tool to pull the handle on the next sliding door. I was back up to full speed. The X8 was loaded. I just needed to chamber the first round. Normally a simple task, but my arms could not remain steady, while I ran. The side of the helmet slide off the gun's handle. I focused on the task. Finally I managed to grip the ear piece on the slider. Pulling back to lift the first bullet up, I used my foot to open the next door, as the assault weapon became ready to fire.

Lifting my head up, I saw them. They were bringing their guns to bear on me. Diving, I swung the helmet up towards my head. Triggers were pulled at the same time. Shots crossed between each other. I could hear one bullet tear through the air by my ear. The next hit the helmet, and crashed it onto my head. Blinded, I fired as I flew forward. As soon as I touched the floor, I began to roll. The train was being destroyed around me. I felt hits to my back, arm, and shoulder. The body armor held, but each area hit, it would be severely weakened. I wiggled in between the benches. Individually, the seats would not stand up to gunfire. However, the several between me and my attackers, supplied some cover. I reloaded. These soldiers had protective vests and helmets, but only cloth covered their limbs. I kept low, firing beneath the benches. Legs and feet exploded. Men fell as bones shattered and flesh was torn away. The rest of the men leapt on to the benches, taking away my line of fire. I was pinned down. I wasn't carrying any explosives. Elise had them all. My options were few.

A stream of smoke flew towards the guards; smoke bomb. Then a few other cylinders followed; concussion grenades. Elise called out to me, then unleashed her X8. The first grenade popped. I scrambled into the walkway. Sending a burst behind me, I crawled out. Elise slid the door behind me. She showed me the remote controlled bombs, as she threw one under a bench. We took off back to the front of the train. She tossed out a few more grenades, on our way. Entering the lead car, Elise turned back to me: "There's video monitors in the cockpit. We can watch the whole train from there!" As she was talking, I saw it in the distance. The heli-Jet was heading towards us. The aircraft could easily destroy the train and track. "They're gonna blow the train! We gotta get out!" Elise grasped my arm. "No! This track is too valuable! This is the only one that heads north. Any damage to the track, and the executives have to travel through the city!" I pointed to the Heli-Jet: "They can fly!" Elise shook her head. "No! Those things are too unsafe! They've built 20 of them, and they've only got 2 working right now! My dad didn't even want to be around those things when they were taking off or landing!" We stumbled forward as the train began to slow. Elise pulled away and headed for the Cockpit. I dug the rocket launcher from her back pack. The Heli-Jet headed towards us, but then turned and passed. Through the front window, I could see it fly towards the building we were heading to. The train was still slowing down, as Elise began to rip open access panels, under the train's controls. The Heli-Jet hovered over the roof. Its bomb bay doors opened. Heavy armed paratroops slid down on ropes. Elise kept working as she spoke." They'll take us at the next station. They'll bring the train in slowly and hit us from all sides once we stop." We both knew we were dead if that happened. She continued: "Fortunately, I started training to be a driver of one of these things. My dad thought it would be a way around security detail. These things are set up to run on electricity and remotely. But they have back up diesel engines, for when the power grid goes down. If I can unhook the electric and start the motor, we'll be in control." We were nearing the next station. In the video monitors I could that the soldiers had not moved from the car, we left them in. There was a rumble beneath my feet. "Ah Hah! Got the motor started and found the electric switch!" Elise smiled up at me. Then her expression changed. "Once they see us speed up, they'll shoot this thing all to shit. This front cone, actually has some armor, so it's our best chance." I nodded my head and snapped my helmet on securely. "Are you ready?" "Does it matter?" Elise smiled with: "No, not really"

Elise ripped a cord out. I shoved the throttle forward. The train sputtered and shook, as a new power source took over. The exterior cameras showed puffs of black smoke exiting either side of the front car. Slowly, we began to pick up speed. Closing in on the station, soldiers could be seen scrambling. We had messed up their plan. Some were trying to block the tracks, while others were setting up firing positions. A bullet impacted the front windshield. I threw myself on top of Elise. We wrapped up on to each other, as we drove into the station. The train became alive with the impact of bullets. The interior of the passenger car was a fog of debris and shrapnel. We slammed into the control board, as the train impacted the blockade. I was knocked off Elise as we lifted off the tracks. Boards and dust broke through the windshield onto us. The car leaned, as it was airborne. I was tossed back over Elise, as the train crashed back on the track. The impact set off the bomb remote. The howl of the explosion roared over us. Somehow, an exterior camera was still operating. I watched as the back end of the train freed itself from the track. Turning, twisting and rolling, the cars left a trail of carnage as the crashed into man and machine.

We emerged out of the other side of the station. All electronics died at this point. The diesel motor still pushed the train, but it sounded sick. It had taken a few rounds, but nothing compared to the passenger cabin. The wind shrieked as it passed though the uncountable holes. I checked us for injuries. Shockingly, nothing had gotten through our armor. Elise smiled and kissed me, but I knew we could not celebrate. I sprung up and made for our backpacks. They had both taken numerous hits. We had lost some supplies, but I wasn't sure how much. Then another sound drowned out the diesel and wind. There was a Heli-Jet above us.

There was impact on the roof. Men were being dropped down. I pulled up my X8 and fired into the ceiling. Elise joined my barrage. Bodies could be heard falling over the car. Then bullets came back at us. I was blown off my feet. Tumbling down the walkway, I lost grip of the X8. A soldier came through the train's open cockpit and caught Elise in the back. A man broke through the ceiling, in front of me. I pulled an automatic 9mm and sprayed him and a man who followed him. They were well armored. Twenty rounds left them injured, but alive. I made it to my feet and attacked. I took my empty gun and hammered it into the first soldier face. As he fell, I leapt over to the next man. I grasp upon his rifle, but he caught me with a blow to the helmet. My left elbow smashed him in the jaw. Taking ahold of him, I spun and threw him on to a broken bench. I was seized by the waste and pulled back to the ground. Charges blew off the sliding doors, and men swung in on ropes. Thrown down on my back, my view came to Elise as she held a handgun under a man's chin. His face became a thousand red drops. She pulled a concussion grenade and tossed it over me. There was flash. The shock wave blew the soldiers back out the opening, they had just come through. I was rolled up in between two guards. I found their necks with each of my hands. I squeezed. They became frantic. Their limbs attacked wildly. I absorbed continuous blows. I fought to hold my grip, as each pawed at me. One managed to free his knife. His strength was leaving him as he raised it. I watched his hand waver in the air. Finally, it dropped.

The sound of the Heli-Jet was different because it had changed positions. It was flying beside us. A fifty caliber Gatling gun was about to brought down on us. They had made a mistake. They allowed themselves to get close to me, after they had given me an assault rifle. I set it through a window hole, and aimed it at the pilot. The windshield was sturdy. The first shots bounced off. The steady stream had an effect, though. The aircraft shook, as the pilot reacted to the fracturing Plexiglas before him. The operator of the Gatling fell. The cannon fired as pulled on it. It ripped into the car behind us. The stream of metal sliced off the roof of the transport. The windshield was battered, but it held up through my entire magazine. I watched the soldier behind the mini-cannon steady himself as I dropped the clipped out. I pulled more ammunition from a corpse behind me. The Gatling gun came back to bear upon us. I fired. The windshield gave way. The dying pilot, pulled back on the stick. The Heli-Jet dove away and spiraled down to the earth. Another Heli-Jet emerged. This one was in attack formation. Elise readied the rocket launcher. She had two shots. The first missile screams out its tube. The second followed from beneath. The aircraft jerked to the right, to avoid the first. It veered right into the path of the second. The Heli-Jet became a cloud of fire, smoked, and red hot metal.

There was no one left to kill. We were alone on the train, with only bodies. Elise and I came together in a tight embrace. I kissed her passionately, thrilled that we were alive. Only then, did we both realize how much pain we were in. Our armor had been battered, and so had our bodies underneath it. We were both bleeding. Joints were swelling up and bruises were forming. We seemed to have made it through with flesh and muscle wounds. We were not safe. There was another station ahead of us. Our armor was useless, and most of our weapons were spent. Elise tried to smile as she motioned towards the dead soldiers: "I'm sure our friends here wouldn't mind if we borrowed some of their stuff." We would rearm and hope that adrenaline and pure stubbornness would get us through the next trial. Elise leaned up and kissed me. "C'mon, I'll let you watch me change. You need to enjoy the view now, before everything gets too blue and purple." She turned to get to work.

There had been something bothering me. It was a feeling that I had been fighting for days. Finally, I couldn't lie to myself anymore. "How much did it cost?" The question froze Elise. Her reaction was too dramatic for the confused look, she attempted when she turned around. She wouldn't have reacted so suddenly, if she had really thought it was too vague a question. Elise knew I had figured it out. Too many events had lined up just right for us. We shouldn't be alive. We wouldn't be, if this was real. It had all played out like an adventure story. Elise wanted to play confused. She was silent as she fought to find the words to deny me. The connection we had, was still intact. I didn't need to explain my evidence. A look of disappointed, surrender came over her face. "On the other side of the stream, there isn't a monetary system, like there is here. However, it would translate to very expensive..... This isn't a simple little dream sequence. It is more real, than you might think. There is no timeframe set. It can end at any time, or it can go on for decades. You are in full control of your own mind and I am in control of mine. I've been here for years..... There's nothing preordained. There are certain situations set up, but how they play out is based on what we do. There are measures taken to ensure we have a chance to succeed, but it is not guaranteed. We could have easily been dead by now. If we don't do anything, before we get to the next station, they'll kill us there. "

It would be a lie to say I had questions. I wanted to have questions, but I didn't even know how to start to even ask. The best I could do was: "Why?"

".......Emotions and physical sensations don't exist on the other side of the stream...This is the only way too...too feel alive...."

I don't know what I was feeling. Maybe you could call it shock. After my suspicion had been confirmed, I didn't know how to handle it.

The passenger car, actually seemed quiet as we stood there. Elise seemed to be waiting for a question. I had nothing at that moment. Finally, she peered around me. She approached me cautiously. "Will you hold me while it happens?" I turned to look through the front of the train. The next station was off in the distance, but we would be there soon. I knew what Elise meant. Just being aware of the game, didn't mean it would end, and there were no time outs. It was being played, whether we participated or not. There would be guards waiting for us at the station. They were there to kill us. I turned back to Elise. She was easing closer: "Please...whatever you think... This is real for me."

I pulled the clip out of the rifle, and checked the ammo count. "We need to get our body armor changed and inventory the guns." Elise gave me a questioning look. The best answer I had was: "Let's see how it ends."

Maybe, one day, I'll get the chance to tell you what happens........

The End. The Leasing Agency. A story by Chad Lundy, writing as C.G. Edwin. Copyright 2014 Larry Chad Lundy. C. G. Edwin will be my pen name. A very special thanks goes to LaDonna Gleason for her help with this story. Her feedback on the previous drafts of this tale were instrumental in improvements that were made. Whatever the quality of this work, it is undeniably better due to her suggestions. It is my wish to have her involved in every writing project I take on in the future. And it is my hope that she will have the available time and interest to take a larger role in those projects. There are numerous people who I would like to dedicate this story too. The list begins with my wonderful and inspiring mother, Patsy. She is truly my hero, my role model, and my friend. There, of course, is also my son, Diego. His arrival in my life, is the strongest evidence I have for a higher power. I can only describe his presence as a blessing. My grandfather's, Edwin and C.G., embody the man I strive to be. Hopefully, one day, I will achieve the example they laid out for me. The other women in my family, that treated me as a son: my grandmother's, Libba and Jewel, along with my Aunt Marsha. I am eternally grateful for maternal love that I have been shown. My two, biological, little sisters that are so precious to me: Amber and Ashlee. Although Amber may be, technically, a cousin, I claim her as a sister. And even though it would be in her best interests to hide her association with me, she claims me too. Ashlee, even though we were raised in different houses, I reject any "Half" qualifier added to our siblinghood. I also have the coolest Uncle (Gary) and Aunt (Laura) in the world. There is also the entire Gleason family. I followed Jason home, as a weird, shy little kid, and was welcomed in as a member of family. I gained two more amazing parents with: Mr. and Mrs. G., the brothers I always needed with Jason and Jeremy, and big sister with Shell. Then Jason and Jeremy managed to land LaDonna and Sarah as wives. Don't ask me how they pulled it off(Probably involved Witch Doctors and Hypnotism), I am just thankful for the two more amazing sisters. And as the family expanded with the addition of some great nephews, the whole clan has continued to keep me around. Which is pretty amazing considering that all I bring to the table, is the occasional comic relief.

There are so many people in my life that deserve to be recognized; even more than I've listed in the prior paragraph. I haven't touched on the romantic loves of my life. The truth is, that this work is not worthy of them. I will continue to work to improve my craft. So that one day I may produce a story that is appropriate for that dedication. There wasn't the same visible activity, as we approached this next station. Dressed in our new armor and armed with our new guns, Elise and I crouched in the cockpit. Elise leaned over towards me."Ben, there's something you should know.""What?""I'm not the Alien. I'm the rental." Copyright 2014 Larry Chad Lundy